Mark and Bryon were like brothers. Mark was golden-eyed, golden-haired, and amoral. Playboy Bryon was dark-haired and passionate. He joined his "brother" in gang warfare in their slum neighborhood. Then the year he was sixteen, things changed for Bryon. A sudden death. Drugs. Booze. Betrayal. When he was younger he didn't have to confront anybody. That was then. . . .

S. E. HINTON wrote *The Outsiders* as a teenager, telling it as it was and how a seventeen-year-old saw gang culture. A few years later S. E. Hinton examined the same area and people to find another exciting and sometimes terrifying story of conflict and rebellion between slum kids and the upper-middle class.

THE LAUREL-LEAF LIBRARY brings together under a single imprint outstanding works of fiction and nonfiction particularly suitable for young adult readers, both in and out of the classroom. This series is under the editorship of M. Jerry Weiss, Distinguished Professor of Communications, Jersey City State College; Charles F. Reasoner, Professor of Elementary Education, New York University; and Carolyn W. Carmichael, Associate Professor, Dept. of Communication Sciences, Kean College of New Jersey.

that was then, this is now

S. E. Hinton

FOR DAVID

Published by
Dell Publishing Co., Inc.
1 Dag Hammarskjold Plaza
New York, N.Y. 10017
Copyright © 1971 by S. E. Hinton
All rights reserved. For information
address The Viking Press, Inc.
New York, N.Y. 10022
Laurel-Leaf Library ® TM 766734,
Dell Publishing Co., Inc.
This edition published by arrangement
with The Viking Press, Inc.

Printed in the United States of America
First Laurel printing—March 1972
Second Laurel printing—April 1972
Third Laurel printing—August 1972
Fourth Laurel printing—October 1972
Fifth Laurel printing—June 1973
Sixth Laurel printing—October 1973
Seventh Laurel printing—June 1974
Eighth Laurel printing—August 1974

ONE

Mark and me went down to the bar/pool hall about two or three blocks from where we lived with the sole intention of making some money. We'd done that before. I was a really good pool player, especially for being just sixteen years old, and, what's more, I look like a baby-faced kid who wouldn't know one ball from another. This, and the way Mark set me up, helped me hustle a lot of pool games. The bad deal is, it's against the law to be in this pool hall if you're under age, because of the adjoining bar. The good deal is, the bartender and owner was a good friend of mine, being the older brother of this chick I used to like. When this chick and me broke up, I still stayed friends with her brother, which is unusual in cases like that. Charlie, the bartender, was just twenty-two, but he had a tough reputation and kept order real good. We lived in kind of a rough part of town and some pretty wild things went on in Charlie's Bar.

I looked around for a plainclothes cop when we went in—I can always tell a cop—but didn't find one, so I went up to the bar and hopped on a barstool.

"Give me a beer," I said, and Charlie, who was cleaning glasses just like every bartender you ever see, gave me a dirty look instead. "O.K.," I said brightly, "a Coke."

"Your credit ain't so hot, Bryon," Charlie said. "You got cash?"

"A dime—for cryin' out loud! Can't you let me charge a dime Coke?"

"Cokes are fifteen cents, and you already got three dollars worth of Cokes charged here, and if you don't pay up this month I'll have to beat it out of you." He said this real friendly-like, but he meant it. We were friends, but Charlie was a businessman too.

"I'll pay up," I assured him. "Don't worry."

Charlie gave me a lopsided grin. "I ain't worried, kid. You're the one who should be worried."

I was, to tell the truth. Charlie was a big, tough

guy so a three-dollar beating up was something to worry about.

"Hey, Mark," Charlie called, "there ain't nobody here to hustle."

Mark, who had been scouting out the two guys playing pool, came up and sat down next to me. "Yeah, that's the truth."

"It's just as well," Charlie said. "You guys are going to get in real bad trouble one of these days. Some guy's going to get hacked off when he finds out what you're doin', and you're gonna get a pool stick rammed down your throats."

"No we ain't," Mark said. "Give me a Coke, Charlie."

"We don't have any credit," I said glumly.

Mark stared at Charlie disbelievingly. "You got to be kiddin'. Man, when did we ever not pay our bill?"

"Last month."

"You said you'd add it on to this month's. That's what you said. So I don't see why you can't add twenty cents to that."

"Thirty cents," corrected Charlie. "And, like I just told Bryon, if I don't get that money pretty soon, I'm going to take it out of a couple of hides."

"I'll get you the money tomorrow if you give us the Cokes right now."

"O.K." Charlie gave in to Mark. Almost everybody does. It was a gift he had, a gift for getting away with things. He could talk anyone into anything. "But if I don't get the money by tomorrow, I'll come looking for you."

I got chilled. I had heard Charlie say that to another guy once. I also saw the guy after Charlie found him. But if Mark said he'd have three dollars by tomorrow, he'd have it.

"Speaking of looking for you," Charlie continued, "the true flower child was in here asking for you."

"M&M?" Mark asked. "What did he want?"

"How would I know? Man, that is a weird kid. Nice guy, but weird."

"Yeah," Mark said. "I guess it would be hard to be a hippie in a hood's part of town."

"Speak for yourself, man," Charlie said. "This part of town don't make nobody a hood."

"You're right," Mark said. "But I really sounded profound there for a minute, huh?"

Charlie just gave him a funny look and got us the Cokes. It was later in the evening now, and some more customers came in, so Charlie quit talking to us. It got pretty busy.

"Where are you gonna get three dollars?" I asked Mark.

He finished off his Coke. "I don't know."

That bugged the heck out of me. Mark was always pulling stunts like that. I ought to know; Mark had lived at my house ever since I was ten and he was nine and his parents shot each other in a drunken argument and my old lady felt sorry for him and took him home to live with us. My mother wanted a hundred kids and could have only one, so until she got hold of Mark she had to be content feeding every stray cat that came along. There was no telling how many kids she might have picked up along the line if she could have afforded more than two—me and Mark.

I had been friends with Mark long before he came to live with us. He had lived down the street and it seemed to me that we had always been together. We had never had a fight. We had never even had an argument. In looks, we were complete opposites: I'm a big guy, dark hair and eyes—the kind who looks like a Saint Bernard puppy, which I don't mind as most chicks cannot resist a Saint Bernard puppy. Mark was small and compact, with strange golden eyes and hair to match and a grin like a friendly lion. He was much stronger than he looked—he could tie me in arm wrestling. He was my best friend and we were like brothers.

"Let's go look for M&M," Mark said abruptly and we left. It was dark outside and seemed a little chilly. This was probably because school had just started, and it always seems like fall when school starts, even if it's hot. Charlie's Bar was on a real crummy street with a lot of other bars whose bartenders kicked us out when we strolled in, a movie house, a drugstore, and a second-hand clothes store that always had a sign in the window saying "We Buy Almost Anything"—and from the looks of their clothes, they did. When my old lady went into the hospital, we got so low on money that I bought some clothes there. It's pretty lousy, buying used clothes.

We found M&M in the drugstore reading *Newsweek*, which shows what a weird kid he was since there were plenty of skin mags and things to read. A little kid like him shouldn't be reading that junk, I know, but he should at least want to.

"Hey, Charlie said you was lookin' for us," Mark greeted him.

M&M looked up at him. "Yeah. How you guys doin'?"

M&M was the most serious guy I knew. He always had this wide-eyed, intent, trusting look on his face, but sometimes he smiled, and when he did it was really great. He was an awful nice kid even if he was a little strange. He had big gray eyes—the kind you see on war-orphan posters—and charcoal-colored hair down past his ears and down to his eyebrows. He probably would have grown a beard except thirteen was too young for it. He always wore an old Army jacket that was too big for him and went barefoot even after it started getting cold. Then his father got fed up with it and M&M got a pair of moccasins. He had a metal peace symbol hanging around his neck on a piece of rawhide string, and he got his nickname from his addiction to M&M's, the kind of chocolate candy that melts in your mouth and not in your hand. For years I'd never seen M&M without a bag of that candy. I don't know how he ate those things all day long, day after day. If I did that, my face would break out like nothing you've ever seen.

"You want an M&M?" He held out a bag toward us. I shook my head, but Mark took one, just to be polite, since he didn't like sweet stuff. "You wanted to see us for something?" Mark reminded him.

"Yeah, I did, but I forgot what for." He was like that. Real absent-minded. "My sister's home," he added as an afterthought.

"No kiddin'?" asked Mark tactfully, thumbing through a *Playboy*. "Which one?"

M&M had a million brothers and sisters, most of them younger. They all looked alike and it was really funny to see him out somewhere with four or five little carbon copies—with dark hair and big serious eyes—hanging all over him. If I had to be a baby-sitter day and night, I'd lose my temper and kill one of those brats, but then, M&M never lost his temper.

"My older sister, Cathy. You know."

"Yeah, I remember," I said, only I didn't remember too well. "Where's she been?"

"She went to a private school last year and this summer. She's been staying with my aunt. She had to come home, though, because she ran out of money. She paid for it all with her own bread."

"Must be smart," I said. I couldn't remember what she looked like; I had never paid any attention to her. "She as smart as you?"

"No," M&M said, still reading. He wasn't bragging, he was telling the truth. He was a very honest kid.

"Let's go over to the bowling alley," Mark suggested. The drugstore wasn't exactly jumping with action. It was a school night and nobody was hanging around. "You come too, M&M."

It was a long walk to the bowling alley, and I wished for the hundredth time I had a car. I had to walk everywhere I went. As if he'd read my mind, which he was in the habit of doing, Mark said, "I could hot-wire us a car."

"That's a bad thing to do," M&M said. "Taking something that doesn't belong to you."

"It ain't stealin'," Mark said. "It's borrowin'."

"Yeah, well, you're on probation now for 'borrowing,' so I don't think it's such a great idea," I said.

Mark could hot-wire anything, and ever since he was twelve years old he had hot-wired cars and driven them. He had never had an accident, but he finally got caught at it, so now once a week he had to go downtown on his school lunch hour to see his probation officer and tell him how he was never going to steal cars any more. I had been worried at first, afraid they were going to take Mark and put him in a boys' home since he wasn't really my brother and didn't have a family. I was worried about Mark being locked up. I didn't need to. Mark always came through everything untouched, unworried, unaffected.

"O.K." Mark shrugged. "Don't get shook, Bryon."

"Bryon," M&M said suddenly, "were you named after the lord?"

"What?" I said, stunned. For a minute I thought he meant God.

"Lord Bryon, were you named after him?"

The poor kid had *Byron* and *Bryon* mixed up. I decided to string him along. "Yeah, I was."

"Was there a Lord Bryon?" Mark said. "Hey, that's cool." He paused. "I guess it's cool. What'd this guy do, anyway?"

"Can't tell you in front of the kid," I answered.

M&M shook his head. "He wrote poetry. He wrote long, old poems. You ought to write poetry, just to keep up the tradition of the Bryons."

"You ought to keep your mouth shut," I replied, "before I keep up the tradition of punching wise guys in the mouth."

M&M looked up at me, and I realized from his hurt, puzzled look that he hadn't been trying to be smart. So I punched him on the shoulder and said, "O.K., I'll write poetry. How's this?" and I recited a dirty limerick I'd heard somewhere. It made him laugh and turn red at the same time. Mark thought I had made it up, and said, "Hey, that was pretty good. Can you just pop them off like that?"

I only shrugged and said, "Sometimes," because then I'd take credit whether or not it was really due me. I was like that. I'd also lie if I really thought I could get away with it, especially to girls. Like telling them I loved them and junk, when I didn't. I had a rep as a lady-killer—a hustler. I kept up the old Lord Byron tradition in one way. Sometimes I'd get to feeling bad thinking about how rotten I treated some of these chicks, but most of the time it didn't even bother me.

"M&M, old buddy," Mark was saying, putting his arm across M&M's shoulders, "I was wondering if you might be able to loan your best friend some money."

"You ain't my best friend," M&M said with that disarming honesty, "but how much do you want?"

"Three bucks."

"I got fifty cents." M&M reached into his jeans pocket and pulled out a couple of quarters. "Here."

"Forget it," I said. Me and Mark looked at each other and shook our heads. M&M was unbelievable.

"It's O.K. I'll get fifty cents again next week, for baby-sitting."

"Is that all you get paid for watching all those kids? Fifty cents?" I couldn't get over it. Fifty cents a week?

"I think it's enough. I don't mind taking care of the kids. Who's going to do it if I don't. Both my parents work, so they can't do it. Anyway, I like my family. When I get married I'm going to have at least nine or ten kids."

"There goes the population explosion," Mark said.

"Well, now that your sister's home she can do a lot of the baby-sitting," I said, trying to be helpful. M&M could tell we thought he was crazy.

"Cathy's got a job after school; she can't help. I don't know what I have to do to convince you that I don't mind it."

"O.K., O.K., I'm convinced." I was also tired of the subject and I had got to worrying about how we were going to get three dollars before tomorrow. Charlie didn't get his rough rep or his bar by being nice to people, especially ones who couldn't pay their bills.

By the time we got to the bowling alley it was ten o'clock. There weren't many people there. Mark and I watched a few games while M&M stared into a package of M&M's. I finally got bugged about it and asked him what in the Sam Hill was he doing.

"Take a look." He handed me the package, which was open at the top. "Put it right up to your eye."

I did, and all I saw was a bunch of candy.

"It's beautiful, ain't it?" asked M&M. "I mean, look at all the different colors."

"Yeah," I agreed, thinking, If I didn't know this kid better I'd say he was high.

"Let me look," said Mark, so I handed him the package. "Hey, this is groovy. Look at all the colors." He gave the candy back to M&M, looked at me, and shrugged.

M&M got up. "I gotta go home now. I'll see you guys later."

"We just got here," Mark objected.

"Yeah, well, I just came along for the walk, and now I gotta go home."

I watched him leave. "The kid's weird," I said. "That's all there is to it."

Mark lit up a cigarette, our last one, so we had to pass it back and forth. "I know, but I still get a kick out of him. Come on, let's go catch up with him. There ain't nothin' to do around here."

Outside I spotted M&M at the corner. There were three guys trailing him. When you see something like that around here you know right away somebody is about to get jumped. In this case, it was M&M.

"Come on," Mark said, and we cut through an alley so as to come up behind those guys.

Three against three. The odds would have been even except that M&M was one of those nonviolent types who practiced what he preached, and me and Mark weren't carrying weapons. We slowed down to a walk when we came to the end of the alley. I could hear the voices of the three guys who were following M&M, and I recognized one of them.

"Hey, flower child, turn around." They were taunting him, but M&M just kept right on moving.

"It's Shepard," Mark whispered to me. We were waiting at the end of the alley for them to come by. They didn't. They must have had M&M up against the wall. We could hear them.

"Hey, hippie, don't you answer when you're spoken to? That ain't nice."

"Curly, why don't you leave me alone?" M&M sounded very patient. I moved over to the other side of the alley just in time to see Curly pull out a switchblade and reach over and cut through the rawhide string on M&M's peace medal. It fell to the ground. M&M reached down to pick it up, and Curly brought his knee up sharply and hit M&M in the face.

Me and Mark looked at each other, and Mark flashed me a grin. We both liked fights. We ran out and jumped on them, and the one we didn't get took off, which was a wise thing for him to do. Since we had surprised them, it wasn't too hard to get them pinned. I had Curly Shepard in a stranglehold with one arm twisted behind his back, while Mark had the other guy pinned on the ground.

"How'd you like a broken arm, Shepard?" I said through gritted teeth, careful not to loosen my grip. His switchblade had fallen on the sidewalk, but I didn't know what all he might be carrying. He liked to play rough.

"O.K., you proved your point. Let us go, Douglas." Curly said a few more things that I'm not going to repeat. He must have figured out who it was twisting his arm when he saw Mark. Me and Mark were always together. Curly had a special grudge against me anyway. I used to go with his sister; she says she broke up with me, which was the truth, but I was spreading it around that I broke up with her and was giving all kinds of cool reasons. Curly was a little dumb —he belonged to a gang led by his brother Tim and known as the Shepard Gang. Really original. Tim was all right—at least he had a few brains—but I considered Curly a dumb hood. "Look, we didn't hurt him."

That was a lie, because M&M was sitting there against the wall and already his cheek was swelling up and turning purple. He was trying to tie the ends of the rawhide string together and his hands were shaking.

"Let them go," said M&M. "I'm O.K."

I gave Curly's arm an extra twist for good measure and then gave him a shove that almost sent him sprawling. Mark let the other guy up, but when he was almost to his feet, Mark gave him a good swift kick. They left, cussing us out, partly in English and partly in sign language.

Mark was helping M&M up. "Come on, kid," he said easily. "Let's get you home."

The whole side of M&M's face was bruised, but he gave us one of his rare, wistful grins. "Thanks, you guys."

Mark suddenly laughed. "Hey, look what I got." He waved three one-dollar bills at me.

"Where did you get that?" I asked, although I knew good and well where he got it. Mark was very quick; nobody had to teach him how to hot-wire a car—or to pick a pocket.

"It was a donation," Mark said seriously, "for the Cause."

This was an old joke, but M&M fell for it. "What cause?"

"'Cause we owe it to Charlie," Mark said, and M&M almost laughed, but instead winced with pain. I was really feeling good. I could quit worrying about Charlie's beating us up.

Mark suddenly poked me. "You still in the mood for a little action?"

"Sure," I said. Mark motioned toward the next intersection. There was a black guy standing there, waiting for the light to change. "We could jump him," Mark said, but suddenly M&M spoke up.

"You make me sick! You just rescued me from some guys who were going to beat me up because I'm different from them, and now you're going to beat up someone because he's different from you. You think I'm weird—well, you're the weird ones."

Both Mark and I had stopped walking and were staring at M&M. He was really shook up. He was crying. I couldn't have been more stunned if he had begun to dissolve. You don't see guys crying around here, not unless they have a lot better reason than M&M had. He suddenly took off, running, not looking back. I started to take a few steps after him, but Mark caught me by the arm. "Leave him alone," Mark said. "He's just all uptight from getting jumped."

"Yeah," I said. That made sense. That had happened to me before, and I could remember how scared it could get you. Besides, M&M was only a kid, just turned thirteen.

Mark picked something up off the ground. It was M&M's peace medal. It must have dropped off when M&M started running. He hadn't tied the ends of the string together very well.

"Remind me to tell him I have this," Mark said, stuffing the medal and the string in his pocket. "Let's stop by and give this three bucks to Charlie before I buy some cigarettes with it."

"O.K.," I said. I didn't feel quite as good as I had before. I was thinking about what M&M had said about beating up people because they were different. There was a lot of truth to that. The rich kids in town used to drive around over in our part of the city and look for people to beat up. Then a year or so ago a couple of kids got killed in that mess and the fad slowly died out. But there were still gang fights around here and social-club rumbles, and things like Shepard's jumping M&M happened every day. I didn't mind it much, unless I was the one getting mugged. I liked fights.

"Come on," Mark called, "maybe there's somebody to hustle in Charlie's." I grinned and ran to catch up with him. Mark was my best buddy and I loved him like a brother.

TWO

The next afternoon after school Mark and me went downtown to the hospital to see my mother. She had just had a big operation, one that cost a lot of money. We had sold our car, an old Chevy —our TV, a little black-and-white job—and anything else we could find to sell, but we were still short of money. I had been trying for weeks to find a job. Mark scrounged around and came up with some money—I didn't ask him where he got it, and he didn't tell me, so I figured he stole it somewhere. Mark was really bad about stealing things. He stole things and sold them, or stole them and kept them, or stole things and gave them away. It didn't bother me. He was too smart to get caught. He had been stealing things since he was six years old. I wasn't above taking a pack of cigarettes from a drugstore, but that was about it. I was the hustler and Mark was the thief. We were a great pair. One thing about it, though. Mark couldn't see anything wrong with stealing stuff. I could. It didn't much matter to me whether or not Mark was a thief, but I still felt that stealing was wrong—at least it's against the law. I think Mark was only dimly aware of that fact. Stealing was a game to him, something to do for fun and profit, and he was careful not to get caught because that was one of the rules.

So that was how we lived, stealing stuff and selling stuff, trying to save money and eat at the same time. I never thought about it then, but I can see now that it was a pretty rough time for us.

Anyway, Mark and I hitched a ride almost all the way to the hospital. The guy who gave us a ride was a hippie with long hair and a beard and a Volkswagen bus. Those buses are very big with hippies, I don't know why. The guy said his name was Randy and that he went to college in town, majoring in English. I figure he was a pretty brave guy. Mark and I looked like tough guys —the kind who go around jumping hippies, which we had done once before. We had gone over to the city park where the hippies hang out, just to beat up somebody. I wouldn't do it again though. I hadn't realized those guys refuse to fight back, and what happened to the one we got hold of, it made me sick. Mark felt the same way. So after that we left them alone.

Randy was telling us about this really cool house where a bunch of his friends lived, an old house they all rented and everybody who wanted to could live there and groove in peace and good will. I didn't much believe him—there had to be a few sponges in a setup like that—and living with a bunch of people would get on my nerves, especially if they were hairy and dirty. But I was polite and said, "Sounds cool," even though it didn't particularly appeal to me. Mark was interested, though, and asked Randy all kinds of questions about where this place was and who all lived there and if he knew about any other places like that. Mark was interested in lots of things— he knew all about the Old West and was nutty about Warner Brothers' cartoons—so it didn't bug me when he got all excited about hippie living.

When we got out of the bus Randy held up two fingers and said, "Peace," and Mark held up M&M's peace medal, which he was wearing around his neck as a joke, and made a wise-crack. Then we looked at each other and cracked up laughing. But we weren't being hateful; it was just funny.

Mom was glad to see us, but she hadn't been

lacking company. We had the kind of neighborhood where everyone knew everybody else's business, and all the ladies came up to see her, at least two a day. They also brought me and Mark junk like pies and potato salad. I got the pies and Mark took whatever else there was, since he couldn't stand sweet stuff. Cokes and an occasional M&M, just to be polite to M&M, was as much sweet stuff as he'd take. As a result, I was putting on weight—I wasn't in much danger of getting fat since it seemed like I was growing an inch taller a week—and Mark was staying as slight and slender as ever. You'd never guess Mark was as strong as he was by looking at him, but I knew from our wrestling matches that he was as tough as a piece of leather.

As usual, the last thing on Mom's mind was herself. We had no more than got there and got hugged when she started telling us about this poor kid across the hall who never had anybody visiting him.

"How do you know that?" I asked. "There's so many people comin' and goin' around here. How do you know about some kid across the hall?"

"The nurse told me. Poor kid, he's not any older than you and Mark—"

It figured—I mean her finding out about it. If there was a lame dog within three miles, she'd find it. It didn't bug me much though. Thanks to her, I had a brother.

"Bryon, promise me you'll go over and see him."

I frowned. "Look, I don't know the guy. I'm not going to just walk in and say, 'Hi there. Want a visitor? My mother tells me you don't have any.'"

"Bryon," Mom said, "just go talk to him. He won't talk much to the nurses. He's been hurt pretty badly, poor thing."

"I'll go see him," Mark said. "Bryon'll come with me." I gave him a dirty look but he continued, "Who knows, maybe one of us'll end up in the hospital sometime with nobody to come and see us."

That was just the kind of junk my mother eats up, and Mark knew it. When we left I stopped him in the hall. "What's the idea of telling her you were going to go see that kid?"

Mark shrugged. "I am going to. Why not?"

This was typical of Mark as it wasn't typical of anyone else. "Well, *I'm* not going. I'm going down to the snack bar here and get a hamburger. Ain't you hungry?"

Mark shook his head. "Naw. I'll meet you down there later."

I took the elevator to the basement, where the snack bar was. I sat on a stool at the counter— after sitting at the bar at Charlie's I had got used to it—reading the menu over and over, thinking about all the food I'd get if I could. I loved to eat. I could put away more food than anyone I knew. I was five-ten at sixteen and still growing, but I went through my lanky period at fourteen and I had a good build, of which I was proud. I should have gone out for football, I guess, but it didn't much appeal to me. I liked neighborhood football games, but all that practice for the real thing seemed like a bore to me. Besides, I knew I couldn't put up with a coach telling me how to play. I never have been able to accept authority. I don't know why. I figure it was because of this cop—these two cops—who beat me up once when I was thirteen years old. I had gone to the movies with these other guys—I forget where Mark was —and we drank a fifth of cherry vodka in Coke and got drunk. That stuff tasted terrible, but I was a dumb kid and I drank it just to show I was as super-tuff as the rest of them. When the movie was over and I was staggering around alone on the streets in the dark, these two cops picked me up, drove me out to a hill on the other side of town, slapped me around, and left me there. I never forgot it. It didn't stop me from drinking, but it sure ruined any respect I ever had for cops. Yeah, sure there are good cops somewhere. I just never met any. Ever since then I've made it a point to mouth off to cops. That's probably why I never met any good ones.

So I was sitting there, reading the menu, when I heard a voice say, "Can I take your order?" and I looked up at this really cute chick. She gave me a big smile and said, "Hi, Bryon! What are you doing here?" I was racking my brain trying to think where I knew her from; she did seem kind of familiar, so to stall for time I said, "I'm here to see my old lady. She's just getting over an operation. I didn't know you worked here."

"I just started this week. But you knew I just got back, didn't you?"

"Oh, yeah," I said, about to go crazy trying to remember who she was. She had this groovy long dark hair with a sheen to it like charcoal—long hair with bangs just drives me crazy. There aren't too many chicks who can wear their hair like that and still look good. And she had these big, beautiful gray eyes, dark gray with black eyelashes and the eyelashes were really long, but they weren't fake. I am a long-practiced studier of girls, and I can tell about things like that.

"Gosh, you've grown," she said. "You must be a foot taller than when I saw you last."

"Yeah, well, it's been a long time," I said. If I had grown a foot it must have been. "How you been doing?"

"Oh, pretty good. I was lucky to get this job. Listen, give me your order. I'm not supposed to stand around talking to the customers."

"Sure. I'll have a hamburger and a Pepsi."

She took my order and left, and I was about to lose my mind. She couldn't have been someone I had dated—I date a lot of girls, but I was sure I could remember them if I saw them again. Anyway, she seemed friendly, and, after you

break up with someone, she's not usually friendly. She seemed so familiar I could have sworn
I'd seen her recently. Whoever she was, I wanted
to see her again. I had already noted that she
wasn't wearing a boy's ring around her neck, or
any other sign that she was somebody's personal
property—I'm in the habit of looking for things
like that. I have gotten into some tight spots with
boyfriends I didn't even know existed.

"Here's your hamburger."

I looked up at her and she gave me this really
great smile, a smile that lit up her face. I knew
I'd seen that smile recently, and then it struck me
who it was, and I was so surprised that I said it
out loud: "Cathy!"

"Yeah," she said, almost as surprised as I was,
"who'd you think it was?"

"The last time I saw you you had short hair
and braces," I said, forgetting that a lady-killer
should never remind a girl of her gawky age
when she was skinny and ugly, or fat and ugly,
or short-haired with a mouth full of metal.

"Yeah, that's the truth. Bryon, you mean you
didn't recognize me?"

"No, I didn't." I couldn't see why that should
shock her so much. Even back in the days of
braces and short hair we weren't exactly best
friends. I had never paid any attention to her. "I
just recognized you because you look so much
like M&M when you smile."

"I am going to take that as a compliment," she

said, giving me my check. "M&M is a beautiful child and he has a beautiful smile to match his mind."

"He's a good kid," I agreed. She turned to go, and I said, "Wait!" without thinking, so when she turned, I stuttered a little. "I mean—I haven't seen you in a while— I'd like to talk to you some-time—" I really wasn't living up to my self-image. I never stutter.

"All right," she said, "we'll talk sometime."

I wanted to ask when, but didn't. You should never be too eager with chicks. It gives them ideas.

I waited around for Mark, but he didn't show up so I took the elevator back to Mom's floor. I went and looked in the room across from Mom's where that kid was supposed to be. I saw him all right, but no sign of Mark. That kid had been hurt bad. He had bandages around his head and across one eye, both arms in slings, and stitches in his lower lip.

"Hey, are you Bryon?" He looked at me out of his good eye. "Mark said to wait for him here; he'll be right back. He went across the street to the drugstore to buy me some comics."

I could tell from the way he talked that he came from a neighborhood like mine. This was likely—it was a charity hospital. "Come on in," he said. "Pull up a chair."

I did. I didn't know what to say to him.

"You're Mark's brother? You don't look much alike."

For a minute I really felt good about Mark's telling this guy we were brothers. Of course, we didn't look alike—Mark with his gold hair and strange gold eyes and slight, tense body, and me, big and husky with dark brown hair and eyes— so I said, "No, I guess we don't."

"I got a brother—older—we don't look much alike either."

I looked around for a No Smoking sign. "Can I smoke in here?"

"Sure, as long as you don't get caught. Would you mind giving me a few puffs?"

"O.K.," I said. I lit up a cigarette and put it between his lips. When I took it back he said, "Thanks. I haven't had a cigarette in a week. My name's Mike Chambers."

"Mine's Bryon Douglas. Man, you look awful. What happened?" I asked. I was beginning to be glad I had come in after all. It must have been rough, being kept in a hospital that gave you the creeps, with nobody to talk to.

"I got beat up," he said with a wry smile.

I couldn't believe it. I thought he'd been in a car wreck or something. "What does the other guy look like?" I said finally.

"It's a long story," Mike said. "You got time for a long story?"

"Sure," I said. I really do like listening to stuff

that's happened to other people. I guess that's why I like to read.

"Well, if it seems like I'm never going to shut up, just tell me. You and Mark are the first people I've talked to in a long time. There ain't much to say to these nurses." I could see that. What can you say to nurses?

"Well," Mike began, "I always had this soft spot for chicks. I was always making like Sir Galahad, opening doors for them and complimenting even the homely ones, and I beat out a lot of guys better looking than me and they never could figure out why. But it wasn't just a line with me. I guess I'm a sucker—I've been taken a few times, like 'loaning' money to chicks who came on with a sob story—but I'll always believe the best about a girl until I'm proved wrong, which is my own hang up.

"That explains the way I acted that night the gang and me was hanging around the drugstore and this black chick came in to buy some cigarettes. Me, I just see a nice-looking chick with really beautiful eyes, all black and inky-soft. I guess I'm a little funny that way, because Negroes just don't get me all upset. I mean, I can see a black guy and a white chick together, and it sure don't bother me, while most white guys can't stand to see that. Like the gang—the minute she walks in, they get all tensed up because black anyone, chick or otherwise, just don't happen to come around much where I live. I guess she worked downtown and got off late and just stopped in on her way to the bus stop. I think she told me that later. I don't remember too good now.

"So she gets her cigarettes and starts for the door, when a couple of guys block her way. Now the gang I hang with is a pretty good bunch of guys—a lot of heart and only a couple of wise apples in the group—but see, nothin' much had been happenin' and they were bored so they start picking on the chick, calling her Black Beauty and some other choice things. They were really getting rude, and I was feeling sorry for the girl. She kept her eyes down and just said, 'Let me by, please,' real soft-like. The guys started pushing her around, not enough to hurt her but enough to scare her plenty. She just gripped her purse with both hands and tensed all over like she was trying to keep from running, which was pretty smart. Running is just an invitation to be chased, and if she got caught it wouldn't be in a lighted drugstore. The old guy who runs the drugstore had disappeared. He was scared silly of the gang. I don't know why. We never done anything to him.

"When one of the guys grabbed hold of her and really got crude, I got fed up. I went over and said, 'Let her go,' like I meant it. They all looked at me for a while, like they were trying to make up their minds whether or not to jump me. We don't usually go around beating each other up, but it has happened. They finally decided not to. My big brother, he's got a pretty big rep as a tough guy in our neighborhood. He's in jail now, that's why he don't come to see me. It was his rep and not mine that stopped them, because I ain't never been known as a tough guy.

"So they turned her loose and went back to reading comics, and I followed the girl outside. She was looking up and down the street kind of desperate-like, and I knew she'd missed her bus. I said, 'Hey, uh, girl, if you've missed your bus I can give you a ride home.'

"She just kept her eyes down. Finally she said something—but, brother, I'm not going to repeat it. I saw then and there she thought I had evil intentions. I don't blame her. Hell, if I'd had to take what she just did, I'd be sore and suspicious too.

"I said, 'Look, I don't want a pick-up or anything . . .' She gave me a funny look so I added quick, 'Not that you're not real cute or anything —I mean you'll have to stay here another hour to catch the next bus and I'll be leaving and I don't know what those other guys might do.'

"She saw the logic in that, because it was getting dark. Not too many cops come around that area; it's kind of a deserted street. You know how cops are; there's a million over on the Ribbon, making sure the nice kids don't kill each other or run each other down, while we can cut each other's throats and they don't give a damn.

"Finally she said she'd let me drive her home. I had my old Ford parked in the drugstore parking lot. It was really my brother's car but he said I could drive it any time he got busted, which is often. He's a pretty good guy, but if you've got a rep for fighting, somebody's always trying to take you on. The last time that happened, my brother busted a bottle over the guy's head and got charged with assault with a dangerous weapon. He never used weapons before, but he had finally got fed up with the whole routine. It wasn't his first offense, so they sat on him kind of hard.

"Anyway, we get into my Ford, and I can see the poor kid is still scared—she sits hugging the door on her side like she's going to jump out any second. I got a couple of good looks at her; she was real slender, looked like she'd sort of sway in the wind, and her hair was down to her shoulders and it must have been straightened. She had on a yellow dress and yellow shoes and she had her straw purse sitting on her lap. She held onto it with one hand and the door handle with the other. She really was cute.

"I started talking to her about just everything. Would her old lady chew her out because she was late? My old lady did. Man, they never liked anything you did, did they? But still, sometimes you couldn't get along without them. Did she go to school? I did but, boy, it was really a hell of a place to spend all day. I wanted to drop out but the old lady said she'd kill me if I did.

"I kept talking because that's what I do with animals when they're hurt and scared, and pretty soon they get over being scared. I've got a hang up with animals, too.

"I could tell she was beginning to calm down a little, at least she let go of the door handle. I even got her to smile once, I forget what I'd been saying. And then I said, 'I'm sorry about what happened to you back there,' and suddenly she started to cry.

"Man, that got me so shook. Nothing gets me shook like chicks crying." Mike stopped here, and I gave him another drag on my cigarette.

"That's funny," I said. "Chicks crying bore me. Go on, Mike, finish your story."

"Well, I didn't know what to say to her. I finally said, 'Hey, don't cry,' which never does any good. She kept on sobbing and now and then I'd catch a word or two. I got the idea that she was fed up with getting walked all over by white people. I could see that. I get fed up with getting walked over by the fuzz, teachers, my old man, and the upper-class kids at school. So I could see that. Bryon, do you know that my old man keeps my mother from coming to see me? Said I was a dumb kid for ever gettin' into this hospital. So anyway, this chick, she tells me about her problems, and she uses some pretty bad language but nothing I ain't heard before from white chicks. I finally pulled the car over to the curb and reached into my pocket. She sat up straight and got all uptight.

"'What we stoppin' for?' she says, and I said, 'I thought I had a handkerchief, but I guess I don't.' I pulled back out on the street. She looked at me for a minute—I kept staring straight ahead but I could tell she was watching me—and she said, 'Thank you.'

"I drove her home. She lived way out on the north side where most of the blacks live; you know where. It is a pretty lousy neighborhood, about as bad as mine. As I pulled up in front of her house, I could see a bunch of kids hanging around on her porch and in her yard.

"'Well, here you are,' I said, a little nervous. For somebody who'd been practicing in her mind how to get the door open, she was pretty slow about getting out. That's how it seemed to me, anyway. I think she was tired out from crying so much.

"Then there was all these black kids around my car. Some big guy opened the girl's door and pulled her out and said, 'What's the matter, Connie? What happened?' You could tell she'd been crying.

"Then they opened my door and dragged me out. It seemed like there was a hundred black faces staring at me. I guess it was really just about a dozen but it seemed like a hundred. I just stood there, backed up against the car. Talk about scared—man, was I scared. To top it off, the chick had started crying again so she couldn't talk."

Mike paused here for a minute. He was staring off in the distance, and when he started talking again, it was slowly, like he was living the whole thing over again.

"The big guy came around to my side of the car. 'You hurt her, white boy?'

"'No,' I said, and it didn't sound very loud so I cleared my throat and said, 'No, I didn't,' so loud that it sounded like I was shouting. It was real quiet; you could hear somebody's TV from down the street and a dog barking a block away and Connie's soft sobbing. I could even hear my heart pounding in my ears. Then the big guy said, really quiet-like, 'What if we don't believe you?' And I got so scared I was about to cry and said, 'Ask her, huh, just ask her!' The guy called across the car, 'Connie, what you want me to do with this white cat?'

"And real soft—her voice was so soft, just like her eyes—she said, 'Kill the white bastard.'

"And sure enough, they almost did."

There was a long silence. I think Mike had forgotten I was listening to him. Then he took a long breath. "That's how I got here. I must be a dumb kid like the old man says though, because I still don't hate Negroes, least of all Connie. I mean, I can almost see why she did it. Almost."

I shook my head. "That's a rotten thing to happen to anybody."

"It sure is." Mark's voice came from behind me. He had been standing in the doorway, I don't know how long. "Come on, Bryon," he said. "Here's your comics." He tossed a couple of monster comics on the bed.

As we got into the elevator Mark said, "I'm inclined to agree with his old man. That is one stupid guy."

"You mean it?" I said. I had been thinking about Mike's story, and I could see his point about not hating the people who beat him up.

"Yeah, I mean it. Man, if anybody ever hurt me like that I'd hate them for the rest of my life."

I didn't think much about that statement then. But later I would—I still do. I think about it and think about it until I think I'm going crazy.

THREE

I had been hunting all over town for a job. I really needed one, but they're not easy to come by if you're sixteen years old with no experience, no contacts. I finally hit upon a great idea: I would ask Charlie for a job. After all, we were friends. He thought I was a smart kid, and having been one himself, he appreciated them. Besides, I figured I would really dig working in a bar.

Charlie's answer was short and to the point: No.

I was sitting at the bar, smoking a cigarette

and trying to fight down my anger and disappointment. I had been hitchhiking all over town for a week trying to get a job. "Well, why not?" I asked, as soon as I thought I could talk without blowing my stack.

"For one thing, you know how often the plainclothes cops stop in. Do you think they'd let a minor work here? You're lucky you can just come in and sit down. Besides, Bryon, it gets rough in here late at night—Yeah, yeah, you're a rough kid, they all think that, but you'd better just take my word for it that you'd be better off someplace else."

"Like where? There ain't no jobs in this town. I been all over. Don't think this crummy joint ain't last on my list." I was mad.

Charlie din't get upset though, he just grinned. "Byron, you're an honest kid in most ways, but you lie like a dog. Take Mark—I wouldn't trust him around anything that wasn't nailed down, but I'd believe anything he said. I'd trust you with my wife, if I had one. I trust your actions, but I double-check most of your statements. You just think about it, and I think you'll come up with the reason why you haven't got a job before now. You just think about it."

I was too mad to think about it right then, but I promised myself I would later. I listened to everything Charlie said, because he was really smart. He had been a high school dropout, but he could subtract and add in his head quicker than a machine, and he had also read almost everything I had, which was quite a bit of reading. Besides, he'd had it even rougher than me when he was a kid, and now he had his own business and was respected by the cops and the rough guys equally.

"O.K.," I said. "If you trust me so much why don't you let me borrow your car Saturday night?" This was a shot in the dark. I really never expected Charlie to let me borrow his car. But I had been thinking about Cathy quite a bit. I had even called her a couple of times—from a pay phone since we couldn't pay phone bills any more—and there was a dance coming up on Saturday night that I wanted to go to. But I didn't have a car.

"O.K., Bryon, you can borrow my car Saturday. Just bring it back with as much gas in the tank as there was when you took it."

I almost fell off the barstool. "You mean it? Really?"

Charlie gave a short laugh. "Yeah, I mean it. But you get into a wreck, and I'll swear you stole it. And I don't care if you let Mark drive it either. Any kid who's been hot-wiring cars and driving them for as long as he has without an accident, I'll trust with my car."

I didn't know how to say thanks. I've always had trouble thanking people, I don't know why. But Charlie just gave me one of those twisted grins of his, like he knew what my problem was and couldn't care less.

"I'll come by and get it Saturday," I said finally. Charlie said O.K., and I could tell he meant, "Get outa here before I change my mind," so I got. I wanted to get to a phone and call Cathy. For all I knew she already had a date.

She didn't, thank God. But she did ask me where I was going to get a car.

"A friend's loaning me his," I said. "We may be double-dating with Mark. You remember Mark, don't you?"

"Who could forget him?" she said, and something gave me a funny feeling, something about the way she said it. It gave me a funny feeling. "Is this a dressy dance or a dance dance or what?" she asked.

"Casual," I said. "Pants would be O.K. It's just at the school gym. Maybe we could go get a Coke afterward"—but I was thinking, Maybe we'll stop by the park afterward, which is just the way I think.

Mark was surprised when I told him who I had a date with.

"Cathy? M&M's sister? How old is she?"

"Fifteen or sixteen, I guess. You want to double-date? Charlie's loaning me his car." I said this casually, like Charlie loaned me his car every day of the week, but Mark wasn't fooled. He never was, by me. "No kiddin'? How'd you manage that?"

I just shrugged. The truth was, I still didn't know how I had managed that.

"Well," Mark said, "I can't double with you. I already told some guys I'd go stag with them. I thought you would, too. Shoot, you haven't taken out a girl since you broke up with Angela Shepard."

"Yeah, well, if you'd gone with Angela for a while you'd be sour on girls, too. Man, I hate that chick."

"Too bad she can look so good and be so rotten," Mark said sympathetically. He never once said "I told you so." He had tried to tell me a long time ago that Angela was no good, but I hadn't paid any attention. It always seemed like Mark knew the score before I did—but it didn't do me any good. I wouldn't listen to him. I had to find out things for myself.

"Who all you going with?" I asked. We were in the kitchen doing dishes. Mark didn't particularly care for washing dishes, but I just couldn't stand a bunch of dirty dishes piled up in the sink.

"Terry Jones, Williamson, and Curtis."

"Then I'm glad I'm not going with you. I can't stand that Curtis kid."

"Come on, Bryon," Mark said easily. "He's a real nice guy. What'd he ever do to you?"

"He thinks he's so good-looking. That whole family's conceited."

Mark was trying to hide a grin. He was laughing at me. "You know good and well he's not conceited. He can't help it if he's good-looking; to tell the truth, I don't think he knows he is. You're jealous, Bryon, because Angela dumped you to make a play for Curtis, and he was smart enough to leave her alone."

"You can think what you want," I said, but I was almost laughing myself. Mark knew me pretty well. Sometimes that could be irritating, but most of the time it was funny.

I thought Saturday would never come, but it finally did. I hadn't looked forward to a date in a long time. With Angela, after a while our dates either ended in a make-out session or a fight. Both got boring.

I was kind of bothered about what to wear. It was a casual dance, so about anything would be all right, but I was bugged anyway.

I was in the bathroom shaving when Mark popped in. He had been down to Charlie's to pick up the car for me.

"Hey, hey, hey!" He leaned in the doorway, grinning at me. "Take it all off."

"You're just jealous 'cause you only have to shave once every two weeks."

Mark refused to be bugged. "You think I *want* to scrape my face every day? Thanks, but no thanks."

I glanced at him just to check out what he was

wearing. Mark never paid any attention to how he dressed—I wouldn't be surprised if someday he completely forgot he was supposed to have something on and walked out into the street naked—but somehow he was always dressed right for the occasion. He had on a gold sweat shirt and wheat-colored jeans and tennis shoes.

"What are you wearin'?" Mark asked. His voice sounded funny.

I shrugged. "I don't know yet."

Mark turned to leave. "I gotta go now. I'm supposed to meet Terry over at his house. I left the keys in Charlie's car." As he was leaving he called over his shoulder, "I found this shirt out in the street, and it's lying on the bed if you want to see it." I heard the door slam and the sound of his light running steps on the porch.

I finished washing off my face and went into our room. Mark and I shared a bedroom which was pretty small—we have a small house—and it seemed even smaller with our twin beds. One was against each wall and that left only a path about three-feet wide to the closet. I wanted to get a look at this shirt Mark had "found out in the street."

It was real funny—that shirt happened to be just my size and dark blue, which happens to be a good color for me. For a minute I wondered whether he had bought it or stolen it—they were the same thing to Mark—but I decided to forget about it. After all, it's the thought that counts.

Mark's clothes were almost all things I had out-grown. I grinned as I buttoned up the shirt. If Mark really cared about clothes he would steal some, but he didn't. But he knew me well enough to know what I would be thinking about.

If you have two friends in your lifetime, you're lucky. If you have one *good* friend, you're more than lucky.

Charlie's car wasn't anything you'd stop and stare at, but it was decent-looking. I felt funny when I stopped in front of Cathy's house. I had always thought of it as M&M's house, and now I thought of it as Cathy's house. I had never paid any attention to M&M's parents and I was about to go crazy trying to remember if I had ever said anything rude or had got smart with them, but I couldn't remember. If I had, I hoped they wouldn't remember.

Cathy's father opened the door. He said, "Hi, Bryon" friendly enough—I guess as friendly as any father ever greets the kid who's taking out his daughter—so I figured I was safe. M&M was lying on his stomach on the floor reading a book with a little sister sitting on his back pulling his hair. I stepped over him. When M&M was read-ing you could blow up the house around him and he'd never notice. I'm that way myself.

Cathy's mother came from the kitchen wiping her hands on her apron, and in the kitchen some more little kids were fighting over who was going to rinse and who was going to dry.

"Cathy will be ready in a minute," Mrs. Carlson said. "Please sit down, Bryon. We haven't seen you in a while."

"I've been out looking for a job," I said, sitting down on a rubber duck. "Mark and I run into M&M every now and then."

"How can you tell him and Cathy apart?" Mr. Carlson said dryly. "I can't any more."

"Now, Jim . . ." Mrs. Carlson began nervously. "We agreed not to say any more about M&M's hair."

Even his own family called him M&M. I tried to remember for a second what his real name was, but I couldn't think of it. In the silence Cathy screeched, "You give me that brush, you brat!" I stifled a laugh.

"How have you been doing in school, Bryon?" Mrs. Carlson asked. She was pretending she hadn't heard Cathy.

This was the usual routine questioning you go through when you have to talk to your date's parents, but I didn't mind. At Angela's house her mother and her stepfather were always fighting and screaming and throwing things, and sometimes her brothers Tim and Curly would get in on it, and I'd sort of duck flying objects until Angela came out of her room, cussing and throwing things along with the rest of them. So you can see why sitting in the Carlson's front room answering questions wasn't really bothering me.

"I'm doing pretty well in school," I answered.

"Mostly A's and B's." I decided I wouldn't say anything about flunking chemistry. The teacher and I had a personality conflict—and when I want to cause a teacher trouble, you'd better believe I can do it.

"M&M is flunking math and gym," Mr. Carlson said in the same tone he had used when talking about M&M's hair. "How anyone can flunk gym is beyond me."

I could tell that M&M was listening to the conversation but was staring at his book, pretending he wasn't. I understood what he was doing. I have stared at a book pretending I couldn't hear what was going on around me, too. If people think you can't hear them, they talk as if you couldn't. You can hear some pretty neat stuff that way.

"It's not as if M&M was an invalid," Mr. Carlson was saying when Cathy came out of her room.

"I'm ready," she said. She had on a yellow pants outfit that looked real cute on her.

I got up. "O.K., let's go." On the way out she gave M&M a friendly kick.

When we were in the car she said, "I wish Daddy would leave M&M alone. He's so sensitive, it hurts him for Dad to tease him about his hair or bawl him out for his grades. It seems to me they should be glad about his other grades—his English teacher says M&M has the most brilliant mind she's come across in five years of teaching

—and be glad he's never gotten into any kind of trouble, instead of picking at him because of his hair." She sighed. "I guess since M&M and I are the oldest, we're the closest. I guess you know about that though. I forgot you have a brother too."

"Yeah, I know about that," I said. Of course, I never heard Mom gripe about anything Mark did—he could get away with things I wouldn't dare try. I never resented Mark for this. I took it as a matter of fact that Mark was different from other people and was therefore treated differently.

Cathy sighed, "Well, I'm not going to worry about it now. I want to have a good time tonight." She gave me a quick, shy smile. She was sitting close enough for me to put my arm around her, which I did. I was intending to have a good time too.

We could hear the music even before we got there. The band was supposed to be a good one—it was loud enough, which with a dance is at least half the way to being good. I was really proud of having such a cute date, and I was hoping Angela would be there. I wanted to show her up. I'd gone with Angela for months, longer than I'd ever gone with anyone. I wanted to show her that I had no intentions of going back to her. She had been telling everybody that I would. This was after she had made her big play for this Curtis kid and he had acted like he didn't know she was alive. Then she decided she wanted me back. You can imagine how that grabbed me.

The dance was going pretty good when we got there. I liked to arrive a little late, when things were swinging. I saw a bunch of people I knew. Cathy knew a lot of people, too, but not very well. She hadn't dated before she left for school, and I don't think anyone remembered her. She had been a shy, plain kid. Everybody was staring at us, wondering who she was. I was really feeling great. I liked being the center of attention. Cathy winked at me. She dug it, too.

I really liked her. I liked her a lot.

"Hey, Bryon!" It was Mark. I could tell even before I spotted him across the room, waving at us.

"Come on," I said. "Let's go see Mark."

We weaved in and out of the crowd, sometimes stopping to talk. I wasn't too happy when I saw that Mark and Curtis were standing together. Having had one girl ditch me to try for him, I wasn't thrilled with the possibility that it might happen again.

"Hi, Cathy," Mark greeted her. He had been drinking, but I doubt that anyone but me could tell. "I haven't seen you in a long time."

"I haven't been here to see," Cathy answered sensibly.

"I don't think you know Ponyboy Curtis—this is Cathy Carlson."

"Hi," Curtis said. He didn't look too happy. I think he had heard I wasn't crazy about him. He was a little guy, about the same size as Mark only with a better build. I think he thought I was going to pick a fight with him. I didn't want to. I guess he couldn't help what Angela Shepard did, and besides, I'd heard he was a pretty good fighter even though he didn't have the rep of a tough guy.

I watched Cathy. She didn't seem interested in him. The first time Angela saw him her eyes lit up like a tiger's. So I relaxed. "Where'd you get the booze?" I asked Mark, when Cathy couldn't hear.

He grinned. "Out in the car—Terry's car. He's got six six-packs, and only the four of us to drink them. Go out and help yourself. Terry won't mind, he's already passed out in the front seat."

Terry had always been a drinker. I decided I'd go out later and have a couple of cans. Maybe I'd get a couple for Cathy. I hoped she wasn't a very heavy drinker—Angela had got pretty expensive with her constant boozing.

Cathy and I watched Mark and Curtis as they started toward a group of girls. "Mark is a good kid," I said.

"I'd forgotten how beautiful he is," Cathy said. "I know girls who would give their eye teeth for hair that color."

I stopped breathing for a second. Cathy was looking at Mark, and I suddenly felt like I'd swallowed a spoonful of red pepper. I felt cold and hot and sick and mad all at once. I only felt it for a second, only for a second and then it was gone—but sometimes now I wonder how it would be to feel like that all your life. You know what the crummiest feeling you can have is? To hate the person you love best in the world.

"Hi, Bryon." The voice was familiar and I turned around. It was Angela. I just looked at her. She was smiling with that sassy smirk, and I wondered why on earth I'd ever given a damn about her. She was beautiful, little and dark, and, even when suddenly all the girls had long straight hair, hers hung to the middle of her waist in ringlets and curls. It was blue-black and shiny. Maybe all that heavy mass wouldn't look good on just anyone, but Angela had the kind of face that would probably be strikingly beautiful even if she shaved her head. But since I knew her so well, I could ignore the way she looked. "Hi, Angel," I said carelessly. "You here with Curtis?"

I meant to rub it in; I think he was the first guy she ever went after and didn't get. Her face contorted for a second, and she called me a few names and flounced off. She wasn't famous for an even temper.

"Who was that?" Cathy asked. I wondered if she was jealous. I hoped so anyway. "This chick I used to go with," I answered. Cathy glanced indifferently after Angela. "Certainly uses nice language," she remarked. "A real lady."

It hit me that Cathy wasn't jealous of Angela at all—not for her beauty or for having gone with me. She was the first girl I'd dated who wasn't scared some other chick would show her up. I didn't know what to make of it.

In the end, I decided it showed that Cathy had more sense than most girls. I wasn't worried about her liking Mark any more. I can tell when a girl is interested in a guy—like the minute I saw Angela looking at Curtis, I knew—and I could tell Cathy liked Mark just as a friend, as the brother of the guy she was interested in. Cathy liked me. I could tell that already.

She was a good dancer. We danced almost every dance. We were having so much fun I forgot all about going out to Terry's car for some beer. They had a cop there at the dance—they always did—but he was ignoring the kids who were staggering around obviously drunk. He was there just to prevent people from killing each other.

Apparently he wasn't even doing that much, because, suddenly above the music, we heard a scream from the back parking lot. Immediately everyone started running out there to see what was happening. I didn't. I hate people who stand around at an accident and pry and push and peer. I won't even stop to watch a fight if I don't know either guy who's fighting.

"Let's don't go," I said.

Cathy nodded. "O.K."

Just then Curtis pushed his way through the

crowd. He had been one of the fighters, because his face was bruised and his lip was cut. "Bryon!" he yelled when he saw me. "Bryon, come quick! Mark's hurt!"

I went cold. Mark was hurt. I shoved my way through the crowd— I'm a pretty good size and when I shove I get through. There was a circle of people on the parking lot. I shoved through them too. Mark was lying on the ground, unconscious. One side of his face was covered with blood. I knelt beside him.

"Mark?" I said, but he didn't move. He was out cold. I took the end of my shirttail and wiped some of the blood off his face. He was bleeding from a bad gash on the side of his head, but that was the only injury I could see.

Curtis knelt down on the other side of Mark. "Is he all right?"

I shook my head. "Did anyone call an ambulance?"

He nodded. "I think the cop radioed for one."

I remembered the cop. I looked around for him; he had some kid in handcuffs a few feet away and was informing him of his rights.

"Is that the guy who did this?" I asked, and the kid in handcuffs looked over at me. He had heard me.

"Yeah," Curtis said.

I looked straight at that kid and said, "Buddy boy, you are dead. You had just better make up your mind to that. When I get through with you,

you are going to be dead." I meant it. I was mad.
The kid just looked away, like he was indifferent.
But he was shook, I could tell.

"He meant to get *me*," Curtis said. "If that
makes any difference."

"If he'd gotten you, he'd be doing me a favor,"
I said. I didn't really mean it, but I was upset.
Curtis gave me a wry grin, like he understood.
For the first time I felt I could like the guy.
"What happened?"

Curtis shook his head. "I don't know. Mark and
me were out here sitting on the car, not doing a
thing, when this guy shows up and starts in on
me. I don't know why, I ain't never seen the guy
before. Finally he takes a swing at me, so I have
to swing back, and pretty soon we're going at it.
Then this character picks up a beer bottle Mark
had thrown over there in the grass and comes at
me with it. About that time Mark steps in between us and says, 'Hey, come on, man, fight
fair.' The kid just looks at him and, for no reason cracks him across the side of the head with it.
Then the cop shows up. Right in the nick of time,"
he added sarcastically.

When I took another look at the kid in handcuffs, Angela was talking to him. I got the picture. She had got this guy to pick a fight with
Curtis—she was mad at him for ignoring her. I
changed my mind. It would be her I'd get even
with, not that poor dope she had used.

"Do you know Angela Shepard?" I asked Curtis. He shook his head. "No. I know her brothers pretty well, but I've never been around her much."

He was telling the truth. Curtis really didn't know that Angela had been after him. He probably thought I had it in for him for no reason at all.

"What does Angela have to do with this?" he asked.

"I'll tell you later."

Mark moved a little and groaned.

"Mark," I said softly, "listen! Don't move, just lie still. We're going to get you to the hospital."

He opened his eyes. The pupils were so large that I could see only a faint ring of gold around them. I picked up one of his hands. It was ice-cold. He was staring straight ahead and didn't seem to hear or see me. I was worried. "What's wrong with him?"

"Shock," Curtis said. He took off his jacket and put it over Mark. I didn't have one, or I would have too. Mark was still bleeding. I couldn't stop it. It seemed that the ambulance would never get there.

When it finally did, I rode in the back with Mark. At last he seemed to recognize me. "Bryon?" he said, then he sort of laughed and groaned at the same time. "Man, am I hurtin'."

"Keep quiet," I said. I was almost crying, something I hadn't done in years. I was pretty worried.

"Listen, Bryon," Mark went on in a weak voice, "when we get there, at the hospital, stay with me, O.K.?"

"I'm not taking this trip for the ride," I said.

He closed his eyes. "O.K., just stay with me."

At the hospital they put ten stitches in his head. The X ray didn't show a fracture or anything, so they said we could go home. I didn't know how in the world we were going to get home—I'd left Charlie's car at the dance and come to think of it, I'd left Cathy there too. I was a little worried about that, but mostly I was worried about getting Mark home.

He was sitting up, but he was still groggy and the painkiller shots he'd been given made him sleepy and high. He was probably still feeling all that beer he'd drunk at the dance too. He was in bad shape.

I thought about calling a taxi, but as it was I didn't know how I was going to pay for the ambulance. I was rescued unexpectedly by Cathy and Curtis. Any other time I would have been hacked off by the two of them showing up together, but right then I was glad to see them.

"I brought your car," Curtis said. "I figured you wouldn't have a way to get home. Is Mark going home?"

"Yeah, they said for him to stay in bed for a couple of days and to come back in a couple of weeks or so to get the stitches out. Help me get him in the car."

"Hey, hey, hey, Ponyboy!" Mark greeted him. "What are you doin' here?" Curtis and I pulled him to his feet and we each slung an arm across our shoulders.

"Come on, buddy boy," I said. "Time to go home."

Mark tried to walk, but almost fell, and we half-dragged, half-carried him out to the car. We got him stretched out in the back seat and climbed in.

"Hey," I said suddenly, "how'd you start the car without any keys?"

Cathy turned to him too. "Yeah, how did you?"

He was getting red. "I hot-wired it," he said finally. "Mark showed me how to weeks ago."

I almost laughed. That was just like Mark. "Don't make that a habit," I said.

Curtis shook his head. "I never done it before." I finally understood that Mark was right about that Curtis kid—he wasn't stuck up, he was shy.

I dropped him off near his house. I hated to just take Cathy home, but there wasn't much else I could do. Mark was singing to himself in the back seat. He had a good voice, but he had picked a lulu of a song. Cathy pretended not to hear it.

I walked her to the door. "I'm really sorry about the way things turned out," I said.

She grinned. "So am I—but thank goodness Mark isn't hurt any worse than he is. I had a good time, I really did—especially driving to the hospital with Ponyboy."

I looked at her quickly. She was teasing me to make me mad.

"Not really," she continued. "He's not my type —too quiet."

"That's one thing I'm not," I said. I wanted to kiss her, but I never know, some girls will kiss on a first date, some won't. I decided to play it safe and not kiss her. Besides, the porch light was on and there were four or five little faces peering out from behind the front-room curtains.

"I'll call you," I said finally.

By the time I got Mark home the shots had worn off. Sweat was running down his face and I think tears were too. But he gave me his typical grin. "I ain't feelin' so good, Bryon" was the most he'd say. I helped him into the house and got him to bed.

"You going to be able to sleep?" I asked when I turned out the lights.

"I don't think so. Man, have I got a headache. You tired, Bryon?"

"Nope," I said. I was sitting on the bed, leaning back against the wall, smoking a cigarette. The light of the moon was coming in the window and I could see Mark clearly. He had one arm folded under his head and was staring up at the moon.

"Well, if you ain't goin' to sleep, and I ain't, why don't we talk for a while?"

"That's fine by me," I said.

played a kid's version of gang fighting called "Civil War," and then later we had got in on the real thing. We fought with chains and we fought barefisted and we fought Socs and we fought other grease gangs. It was a normal childhood. I used to be able to get all uptight about a fight, look forward to it. Nowadays it was getting a little boring.

Mark had a great memory—better than mine, which is pretty good—and he brought up little goofy things we had done when we were young that I'd forgotten about. Like the time we climbed over the back fence at a drive-in movie and got caught. The drive-in manager put us in the back [of] a pickup truck to take us to the police station, [bu]t we jumped out while he was doing thirty [mil]es an hour. Somehow neither of us was killed. [I] always wondered what that guy thought [whe]n he got to the police station and there was [nobo]dy in his truck.

[We'] d get up on the roof of a two-story shop-[ping c]enter and shoot water pistols at the people below, then have a good time running [th]e cop Mark had so thoughtfully drenched. [alwa]ys had a car in those days, thanks to hot-wiring abilities. We'd take some-looked fast and go to the expressway It was sheer luck that when Mark was [caug]ht doing this, he was alone. I could [b]ooked too.

[Mixe]d up between these episodes were

"Y'know, when I first came around tonight, after that kid cracked me, I was scared stiff. I thought I was dyin', I was so scared. I really felt weird. But after I got to thinkin' you were there with me, I calmed down. Bryon, you're the only family I got, you know that? I mean, your mom's been great to me and everything, but I don't feel like she's really *my* old lady. But I feel like you're my brother. A real one."

Mark had never had a real family. I remember once when we were very young. I had remarked that he didn't look much like his father. And he had said, "He ain't my real father. My real father was a cowboy, here for the rodeo. The old lady said he had gold hair and gold eyes just like mine and that he won all kinds of prizes at the rodeo."

At the time I just thought, Gee, that's great, his real father is a cowboy. When I got older I realized what that meant, that Mark was illegitimate. It had never seemed to bother him. But then, nothing did. Maybe it had, and I just never knew it.

"I must still be high." Mark's voice broke the stillness. "I don't know why I'm blabbering on like this."

"I always think of you as my brother," I said. I saw Mark's face in the moonlight. He was smiling.

FOUR

Mark wasn't feeling any better the next day. When I asked him if his head still hurt he said, "Yeah." That was typical of Mark who never admitted to being in real pain. I called the doctor from a pay phone, and all he said was that Mark would be in pain for a couple of days and that I should keep him quiet and give him aspirin. He was a big help.

I took back Charlie's car and told him what had happened. He didn't seem too interested, but

he was having his own troubles. He'd got his draft notice.

I got home as soon as I could. I hated to leave Mark there all by himself. I didn't know which was bothering him most—the pain in his head or having to stay in bed. He probably would have tried to get up in spite of the doctor's orders, but he couldn't even sit up without getting dizzy. We didn't have the TV any more and Mark couldn't read too well. He couldn't even seem get interested in poker.

"Why don't you read me a book?" he sugge after I had racked my brains trying to th something to do.

"Read you a book?"

"Yeah. Don't you remember when little? You used to read me books all the

Mark was too lazy or too uninterest himself; he had never bothered t read very well in the first place accounted for his poor grades he was every bit as smart as I w

I had read cowboy books t little—we were both going like *Lone Cowboy* by Will tree in the back yard then we'd play cowboys Mark said.

Somehow we spe ing about when

poker games, sometimes drunken ones lasting all night, and pool games—I was a pool hustler at a very early age. And dates and parties and beer blasts on the dry riverbed. We were always with a bunch of guys. Sometimes it was the same bunch for a year or two, then people would drift away—usually if anyone got a steady girl it cut down on a lot of goofing around with the guys—and different people would drift in. But Mark was always the hub of this circle of people, and I was always with Mark.

"We've had some good times, huh, Bryon?" Mark broke the silence. I guess we both had been reminiscing.

"Yeah," I said. I was sitting in my favorite position on the bed, leaning against the wall with my knees up, resting an elbow on my knee, and dangling a cigarette.

"Do you ever get the feeling that the whole thing is changin'? Like somethin' is coming to an end because somethin' else is beginning?"

"Yeah, I know exactly what you mean. Like now I couldn't care less about Angela, and I can remember when she seemed like the most important thing on earth."

"That's it!" Mark said excitedly, forgetting about his head and starting to sit up. He remembered suddenly, because he yelped and lay back down with a rueful grin. "Like we got into those gang fights—it was so important, it was the whole world if we won or lost—and the buddies we had then. We were like brothers, not just you and me, but all of us together. We woulda died for each other then. And now everybody's kinda slipped away, and then we woulda died for each other. Really, man, remember? It was great, we were a bunch of people makin' up one big person, like we totaled up to somethin' when we were together."

"Now we total up to something by ourselves just as easy," I said. I understood exactly what he was talking about. Mark had the habit of thinking the way I did; the difference was that he said it and I usually didn't.

"Yeah, but still, don't you kinda miss that one-for-all, all-for-one routine? It's kinda sad, really, when you get to where you don't need a gang— I mean, like you did before."

"It's kind of a good thing too," I said, "when you know your own personality so you don't need the one the gang makes for you."

"Yeah," Mark sighed. "But there's a difference. I wonder what the difference is?"

"The difference is," I said evenly, "that was then, and this is now."

Mark flashed me that lion-like grin. "Bryon, you are brilliant."

We didn't say much the rest of the afternoon. We were thinking.

Mark missed one day of school. He still wasn't feeling real great by Monday, but I decided I could go anyway. He wasn't sick enough for me to stay home with him.

The fight had made Mark something of a hero, and the whole story was going around school in various versions, all different. Some of them were pretty funny. Everyone was mad at Angela, sympathized with Curtis, who had been in a lot of trouble before and was a kind of folk-hero, and made a big deal out of Mark's stepping in to keep the fight fair. When people asked me what happened, I told them, but I could see that they were going to believe what they wanted to believe and hearing the truth wasn't going to change their minds. People are generally like that.

I was in a funny mood Monday. That talk I had had with Mark really got to me. I felt like I was standing apart from all the rest of the kids and just watching. It was like I could see through them—see what they were thinking and why they did things—and it was really weird.

I went to a big high school. It graduated about seven hundred kids, and the senior class was the smallest class, so you can see how big it really was. Its district included a real crummy part of town—ours—and a pretty ritzy part of town. This can make for problems. It used to anyway, with the Socs beating up the greasers, but in these days, with all that love, peace, and groove stuff, the fights had slacked off. Besides, it was hard now to tell a Soc from a greaser. Now the greasers wore their hair down on their foreheads instead of combed back—this went for Mark and me too—and the Socs were trying to look poor. They wore old jeans and shirts with the shirt-tails out, just like the greasers always had because they couldn't afford anything else. I'll tell you one thing though: what with fringed leather vests and Levi's with classy-store labels in them, those kids were spending as much money to look poor as they used to to look rich. It was crazy.

There was another crazy thing I noticed for the first time that Monday. I'm a smart kid, so I was put in classes with other smart kids. Most of these guys were what we used to call Socs. They were always friendly toward me, and I'd gone to quite a few parties at their houses and dated some of their chicks. All this time I had thought, Well, they like me. I'm big, friendly, wise-guy Bryon, so they like me. Now I saw it clearly. They didn't like me. The truth is they were probably scared of me. But I was a "poor white," and they were "liberals," so I got invited to the parties so everyone could see what hip, hip people they were. I had always wondered why at those parties people were always trying to get me to talk about politics and junk I'd never heard of. I don't keep up on those things. When I read, I like stuff like Hemingway—newspapers bore me. I lead with my left, and that's about as much as I know about Left, Right, and so on. I have a vague notion that the Left is Hippie and the Right is Hick, but I really don't know much else.

Now I knew. That Monday I could see through people and I knew what was going on. I figured if I'd been a black I'd have been twice as popular, but integration in our school wasn't really swinging yet, and there weren't very many Negroes there. These guys would probably have offered me their sisters' hands in marriage if I'd been black. I knew some Negroes, some really cool fighters out in Brumley. I'd have to remember to take a couple along to the next party with me. Then they could talk about the Black Revolution and the Panthers—which they knew as much about as I did Right and Left.

I walked around the whole day laughing to myself. It was just that day—the next day I wondered what had hit me to make me act like that; and when I saw these Soc guys, they were just guys, friends of mine, and of course they asked me to their homes because we were friends—we were in the same English class and we got along. They were sincerely trying to change the world for the better, that was why they talked politics. They wore those clothes because that was their bag. That's what I thought the next day.

But not Monday. That Monday I knew.

Mark got better and went back to school. He went to school for lack of something better to do, because he sure didn't dig it the way I did. We didn't usually see each other much at school; we were never in the same classes. We walked to school together and usually got a ride home together with someone, but lots of times we didn't see each other until we got home.

So when Mark didn't show up for a while one afternoon the following week, I wasn't worried. He could have been any number of places. I didn't happen to guess the right one. He was at the police station.

I didn't know about it until Terry Jones came by. Terry was short, round, and a real nut.

"Bryon!" he yelled as he came running through the front door. "Hey, Bryon, did you hear what happened to Mark?"

I was making a peanut-butter-and-honey sandwich. I didn't get shook because something is always happening to Mark.

"What? And calm down, for Pete's sake. I ain't deaf."

"O.K.," Terry said carelessly. He sat down in a chair and looked around. "Having dinner?"

"Cut it, man. What happened to Mark?"

"Not much. He just got caught driving the principal's car."

I gagged. "What?" I said when I could talk. "He got caught doing what?"

"The principal had to leave school early today for some reason. He gets to his parking place, and no car. And then guess who shows up with it? Your friend and mine, Mark."

"You gotta be kiddin'," I begged. "Man, Terry, tell me you're kiddin'. Mark's on probation now for car stealing."

"That's the reason he was driving it," Terry said. "Can I have a sandwich?"

"Here," I shoved the peanut butter, honey, and bread at him. "Fix it yourself. Only first, if you don't want your head busted, tell me what's going on."

"I happened to be standing around when the aforementioned incident occurred." It figured. Terry was usually standing around. "And I hear Mark explain to the principal while the cops are bein' called that he has to go down to see his probation officer once a week and tell him how he ain't gonna steal no more cars. The deal is, he don't have no way to get downtown—there ain't no buses at that time, he don't have a car, and there ain't enough time to walk since he's on his lunch hour. So he borrows the principal's car, drives down to see the probation officer, and drives back. He's been doing this since school started, and if the principal didn't have to leave early today, he'd be doin' it yet."

"I don't believe it," I said slowly. "He's gonna be in jail for the rest of his life."

"I doubt it," Terry said, starting in on his second sandwich. "The principal was laughing by the time Mark got through talking to him."

I breathed a sigh of relief. Mark would come through. Even this. As if to prove this to me, Mark came strolling in. "Guess where I been? Got anything else to eat?"

"Let me see," I said. "Ah, yes. I see it in a vision—you were at the police station explaining how you had to borrow the principal's car because you had to see your probation officer."

"Terry told you, huh? Well, it's all straightened out now. The probation officer drives down to pick me up from now on. It was just one of those failures to communicate."

Mark sat down across the table from me, eating an apple. He was trying to look ashamed of himself, but it just wasn't coming off. I was trying to look disgusted with him, but that wasn't working either.

"I'm sorry," he said finally.

"No you ain't," I said. We were quiet for a while. Terry got up and left—he must have thought me and Mark were going to have a fight.

"Listen, man," Mark began, but I cut him off.

"Shut up, O.K.? As long as they ain't doin' nothin' to you, it's O.K. I guess you can get away with anything."

Mark leaned back in his chair. The sun came through the small kitchen window and glinted on his eyes, turning them a bright yellow. "I guess so," Mark said. He smiled, like an innocent lion.

FIVE

The first time Mom knew anything about Mark being hurt was when we visited her in the hospital and she saw the stitches in his head. They were real noticeable against his gold hair. She just said, "How did that happen?" And Mark answered, "Fight," and the subject was dropped. That was a good thing about Mom—she'd cry over a dog with a piece of glass in his paw but remained unhysterical when we came home clobbered. About fights, she'd say, "Don't fight at school, you'll get expelled." About drinking, "I'd rather you didn't," so around her we didn't. She didn't know about some of the rest of the stuff we did—the pool games, the poker, the gang fights, the dry river-bed parties—but in that respect she wasn't any different from any other mother. Parents never know what all their kids do. Not in the old days, not now, not tomorrow. It's a law.

We stopped in to see that kid Mike, the one who'd been beaten up so bad. He looked worse than he had before; he said his old man had been in and chewed him out. The doctor had promised him that his father wouldn't be allowed to come to see him any more, but he was still shook.

He looked like a nervous wreck as well as a physical one. "I wish I was dead—or somebody else," he said. You just don't say things like that. I didn't stay long; things like that depress me. Mark stayed on to see if he could cheer up Mike. I wanted to go to the snack bar and see Cathy anyway.

She looked as cute as ever. She said, "Hi, Bryon," not too eager but friendly enough. I had called her a few times in the last couple of weeks and walked to her house to see her, but we hadn't been out. I didn't have a car and Charlie was still so mad about getting his draft notice that I didn't have the nerve to ask him for his car again. As a matter of fact, he was in such a rotten mood that I stayed away from his place altogether. We were friends, and I didn't think he'd ever take his temper out on me, but with big guys, it's safer to be careful.

"I'm on my break now," Cathy said, looking at the clock. This was an invitation for me to buy her a soda, so I said obligingly, "Want a Coke?"

"I knew you'd say that," Cathy said. She came around to my side of the counter and sat down next to me. I never could get over her honesty. Girls are usually careful not to let you know what they're thinking. Cathy hadn't dated before, maybe that was why she was so open. She didn't tell me that about not dating, of course. I found out from M&M. I found out a lot of things from M&M. I have never known anyone so unsuspicious as that little kid. He'd trust Jack the Ripper. He was a believer.

I kept comparing Cathy to Angela, I guess because out of all the girls I've dated—I started at thirteen—they were the two I liked best. I don't know if "like" is the right word for how I felt about Angela. I had been wrapped up in her, I had to see her every day, I had to talk to her ten times a day on the phone; but now, looking back on it, I don't remember ever liking her. Cathy was smart, but Angela knew more. That was strange. They both had guts—I can't stand chicken girls—but in different ways. Cathy wasn't afraid to do what she wanted. Angela wasn't afraid of any boy on earth; Cathy wasn't afraid of any other girl. They were both gutsy in different ways.

My main problem with Cathy was that she liked me—and I wanted her to be crazy about me. I'm like that. I have a very bad ego hang up.

"Guess who called me?" Cathy said. "Ponyboy Curtis. He wanted to go out Friday night."

"No kiddin'," I said, while thinking, I'll murder that guy. "What'd you tell him?"

"I said I was busy. Am I?"

I was stunned again but didn't show it. "You are. I'll pick you up at seven." I had no idea what I was going to pick her up in, or where we'd go after I did pick her up, but I figured I could work that out later.

"We're goin' hustlin'," I told Mark as we walked home, trying to hitch a ride. This time no friendly hippie showed up to give us a lift.

"O.K."

"Tonight—for money."

"You'll need some money to get started with," Mark said, lighting a cigarette.

"I'll get it."

We ran into M&M at the drugstore, and as usual he was chomping on that crazy candy. At least he wasn't staring into the bag like it contained the eighth wonder of the world.

"I need some money," I said, deciding not to beat around the bush. "You got any?"

He looked at me with those serious, war-orphan eyes. "I got five dollars," he said. "I raked some lawns to get it."

I used to think he and Cathy looked an awful lot alike, but not any more. Sure, they both had those big charcoal eyes and matching hair, but Cathy laughed more, her expression usually twinkled with humor. M&M rarely smiled, and he always looked puzzled, serious, and trusting.

"That's a good deal. Can you loan it to me? Just for tonight. I'll pay you back tomorrow."

He pulled out his billfold and took all the money out of it. "Be sure not to forget to give it back tomorrow. I need it. O.K.?"

"Kid, have I ever given you a dirty deal?" I said, winking at Mark.

"No," M&M said, and went back to his magazine. I never could figure that kid out. I liked him though, partly because he was Cathy's brother, partly because he was a good kid, and partly because he had lived to a nice old age in our neighborhood—for a sucker.

Mark had given him back his peace symbol. It hung around his neck on the rawhide string, and M&M kept twisting it absent-mindedly. I wondered if his father still gave him a bad time because of his hair.

We decided to hit Charlie's place first. Charlie grinned and waved at us when we came in, so I figured he was over his bad mood about being drafted.

"Guess what?" he said, just like a kid. It was the first time I'd ever seen him act like a kid. "They're not goin' to take me."

"How come?" Mark asked, plopping down at the bar. "Bad knee from playing football?"

Charlie shook his head. "Naw, because of my police record."

"You got a record?" I said. "I didn't know that. What'dya do?"

"When I was twelve years old I cut a guy's throat. You in here to play pool?"

I still don't know if Charlie was telling the truth or just kidding us, sort of telling us that it was none of our business what his police record was for. Either was possible.

"Yeah, we're here to play pool. Any possibilities?"

Charlie nodded toward the poolroom. "There's a couple of guys in there. I watched them a little; you can take them."

"Good enough," I said, sliding off the stool.

"Hey, wait a minute," Charlie said. We turned. "Would it do any good to tell you to be careful?"

"Nope," said Mark bluntly.

Charlie kind of laughed and sighed at the same time. "I didn't think so."

We played pool until twelve o'clock that night. The two guys we played against were tough characters, out-of-towners from Texas. At first we played partners, me and Mark losing by a couple of balls. Then Mark started his routine about wanting to go home—"Come on, Bryon, you lost all the money you can spare"—while I played the eager kid—"I know I can win the next game."

Then we played singles. I played the better of the two, a weather-beaten guy in his twenties who looked like an ex-con; for all I know he was. I don't know where else he could have picked up his lingo, because he used the worst language I've ever heard, and I've heard plenty.

I was careful not to win at first, and then, when I did start winning, I only made it by a few balls so it'd look like an accident. But once I started winning I didn't quit. By midnight I had twenty-five dollars and fifty cents.

"You're a darn good pool player," Dirty Dave said—he'd told us that was his name—or words to that effect. His friend, who had been standing around drinking beer for the last three hours, mumbled something about being "too good for his own good," but Dirty Dave shut him up.

"Closing time," Charlie said. He didn't have any other customers but us by that time; he had been watching the game for the last hour and a half.

"We're leavin'." Mark was sitting on the table of a booth and drinking a beer. I don't know where he got it, and from the surprised look Charlie gave him, Charlie didn't know where he got it either.

"See ya 'round, kids," the Texans said as they sauntered out. I was busy counting my money and Mark was stretching his legs.

"So the hustler strikes again," Charlie said. "How much did ya get?"

"Enough. Can I borrow your car again some time?"

"I guess so, just as long as you buy gas. Come on, beat it. I got some work to do. Next time you sneak a beer, Golden Boy, you're going to get stomped on."

"I didn't sneak nothing. I simply walked over and drew a beer. I can't help it if you didn't see it. I left a quarter on the cash register."

"You are good at bein' invisible, man, because anybody gets within ten feet of that cash register, I know it."

"You're gettin' blind in your old age," Mark said, apparently not caring if he got stomped on or not. I gave him a warning look, and he obediently shut up. I wasn't taking any chances—we left as soon as we could.

We didn't get far. Two dark shapes stepped out of the alley next to Charlie's and a voice drawled, "Step right into the alley, kiddies."

I froze, because the voice was Dirty Dave's. I thought about making a run for it, but the voice said, "I gotta gun," so I decided not to. I still didn't move. Mark suddenly said, "We don't want to see the alley, we seen it before," and he sounded like he was trying not to laugh.

"We're gonna give you a lesson on why not to hustle pool. Just step into the alley. Now."

I glanced at Mark over my shoulder. He shrugged, like he was saying "What else can we do?" So we walked past the Texans into the al-

ley. I was beginning to shake. I was having vi-
sions of my thumbs being chopped off or my
arms being broken—things like that happen to
hustlers. When we reached the dead end of the
alley, we turned and faced the Texans—the one
guy was holding a gun on us while Dirty Dave
was putting on some brass knuckles. I could just
picture what my face was going to look like when
he got through with me. I suddenly remembered
Mark, who hadn't done anything but get me
started. "Let Mark go," I said, and my voice was
steady. I was surprised—I thought it would be
shaking as bad as I was. "He didn't do nothin'."

Mark said quietly, "I'm not goin' anywhere,"
and Dave said, "You'd better believe it. You were
settin' him up, and when I get through with hustler here, I'm goin' to give you a lesson too."

"Brass knuckles, guns, or whatever," Mark said
in a voice I couldn't even recognize as Mark's,
"you'll know you been in a fight if you tangle
with me."

"I'm really scared, kid," he said. My eyes were
used to the dim light by now; I could see past the
Texans into the street. I was praying for a police
car, something I never thought I'd ever do. Dave
took a step toward me. I backed up against the
alley wall. I was afraid that if I moved to grab
up something to fight with, the other guy would
shoot me.

Just at that moment somebody stepped into
the other end of the alley and a voice said, "Drop

the gun and freeze—I got a sawed-off shotgun here and I'd hate to scatter dirt all over this nice clean alley."

It was Charlie. I never thought I'd be so glad to see anyone.

"Bryon, Mark, come on out of there."

We couldn't resist smirking a little as we walked past the Texans. Even in the dark I could see the anger contorting their faces. It should have warned me, but it didn't.

"Thanks, Charlie," Mark said as we reached him. "You're a real pal."

"I hope you two learned something from this," Charlie began, but before we knew what was happening one of the Texans made a dive for the gun and fired at us. Charlie slammed both of us to the ground, but in an instant Mark freed himself, grabbed up the shotgun Charlie had dropped, and fired back at the Texans, who were scrambling over the alley wall. It all happened so quickly that I was trying to figure out what I was doing on the ground with my ears ringing from the blast before I realized what had taken place.

Mark was swearing and in the dim light he didn't even look like Mark. He looked perfectly capable of murder; his only regret was that he had missed. I didn't have any similar regrets; if he had missed, well, so had they. You can't feel too bad when you could have been dead but aren't.

"You can get off me now, Charlie," I said. Charlie didn't move. I rolled out from under him. "Hey, man, come on," I said. Then, in the white, sickly light from the street lights I saw that there was a neat, perfect hole above Charlie's left eye. He was dead.

I wouldn't talk about what had happened to anyone but Cathy and Mark. The next few weeks it seemed as if I was moving in slow motion while other people were speeded up. Mom came home from the hospital and I flunked chemistry and Angela got married to some creep friend of her brother's. I called Cathy every day. Mark was the one who explained everything to the police. The police were very impressed with Charlie's having saved our lives and all that. They were local cops who had known and liked him anyway. They told us we could have his car. I took it because I figured he would have given it to us if he had had the time.

I guess I was acting pretty strange during those weeks because one day Mark said, "Lookit, man, Charlie knew what kind of people came into his bar—why do you think he kept a shotgun handy? He knew those cowboys had a gun, he knew what kind of a chance he was taking."

"He told us to be careful," I said. I couldn't get it out of my mind, Charlie's warning us about hustling. "He didn't have to try to get us off the hook. Mark—can't you see? This ain't some story,

some TV show, bang! you're dead, big deal. This
is the real thing. Charlie is dead! He was all set
for life, he wasn't gonna get drafted, he had his
business, he was all set, and then we blew it for
him."

"We didn't blow nothing, Bryon. Things happen, that's all there is to it."

"Not things like that," I said.

Mark didn't understand and Cathy did. I
started spending more and more time with
Cathy. Since I had the car, we went for a lot of
drives and got a lot of Cokes together. We were
always talking to each other about the way we
felt—I tried telling her how I felt about Charlie,
about how shook the whole thing had me. She
told me about herself, about how she wanted to
go to college more than anything, about how she
worried about M&M, and about life in a big family, something I wasn't familiar with. She was so
smart, yet she didn't know a lot of things. She
was one of the few really innocent chicks I had
ever run into. But I could talk to her about anything, talk to her better than I could anyone, even
Mark.

After a few weeks we'd drive by the park and
make out for a little while. It was different for
me though, because I had quit thinking only
about myself, quit pushing for all I could get.

Mark was acting strange these days, too. He
would stare at me for long periods of time when

he thought I wasn't watching, like he was trying to find the old Bryon in this stranger, like he was trying to figure out who I was. One night he even almost lost his temper with me when I told him I was going goofing around with Cathy instead of with him. It was as if he felt something slipping and was trying to hang on. I couldn't help him; I was trying to hang on myself.

He even acted like he was jealous of Cathy. In all the years I'd known him, in all the years I'd gone with different girls, he had never acted like that.

I was changing and he wasn't.

SIX

The Texans were finally caught and tried. I had
to go to the trial to testify. Mark did too. He
watched me closely at first—I guess he couldn't
forget that by the time the police had showed
up at Charlie's I had been hysterical. He didn't
have to worry. I went through the whole trial
calm, collected, numb, and empty. I felt like a
tape recorder playing back something it had impersonally recorded. The Texans were sentenced
to life after a trial that didn't last as long as I
thought it would, I guess because there wasn't

any defense. I didn't feel glad, or vengeful, or anything. I really hadn't much cared whether or not they even caught those guys. Charlie was dead, nothing was going to change that.

I tried to figure out what made me so shook up about it. I knew people died, although I still can't see me doin' it. My father had died, so I knew that people close to you died the same as strangers did. I guess I just couldn't see standing there—alive, talking, thinking, breathing, being —one second, and dead the next. It really bothered me. Death by violence isn't the same as dying any other way, accident or disease or old age. It just ain't the same.

That winter Mark and me were kind of celebrities because of our involvement in the trial. We were invited to Soc parties and we were stared at in the halls and even the teachers treated us differently. I just put up with it. Mark kind of enjoyed it. He felt bad about Charlie being dead though, enough to shut up people who tried to get him to talk about it.

Mark and me used to go down to the bar and just sit on the curb across the street and stare at the boarded-up windows. Just sit and stare and not say anything. It's funny how you don't think about people until after they're dead. Or gone.

Mom had to stay in bed for a month, so we were really getting hard up for money. I got to thinking about what Charlie had said when I asked him for a job. I decided I needed a haircut, clean clothes, and a really big change in attitude. I've told you that I don't like authority. This gives people the impression that I'm a smart-aleck kid. I'll admit I'm pretty mouthy. I got to thinking, Who's going to hire a mouthy kid who acts like he already knows it all?

"Even if you do know it all," Mark said one evening while we were sitting on the porch, "you don't have to let them know it."

"Very good idea." I grinned at him. We were getting along better lately—he had given up trying to keep us together the same as we used to be. I know now this must have been a struggle. Branching off from Mark couldn't affect me so much—I was all wrapped up in Cathy. He was on his own. I didn't know how he spent his time when I was with Cathy, and I didn't bother to find out.

"When you go so far as to get a haircut and iron a shirt, I know you're serious. We're really hard up, ain't we, Bryon?"

"Yep. Or hasn't the shortage of food bugged you at all?"

"I don't eat like some people. I'm goin' to start bringin' in some money. You wait and see, buddy, I ain't gonna sponge forever."

This was the first time in all the years that he had lived with us that Mark ever said anything about being dependent on us.

I looked at him quickly, and I wanted to say:

"What do you mean, sponge? We love you and we want you here, and Mark, you're my brother and you've got a right to whatever I've got."

I didn't. I said, "Don't be a ding-a-ling." Now I wish I had told him how much he meant to us, to me and Mom, how he made us seem more like a family. But I never have been able to say things like that, to tell people I loved them, unless it was some nitwit chick I couldn't care less about. So I just gave him a punch on the shoulder. He grinned at me, but absently, like he was thinking of something else.

That night Cathy and I went for a drive. I wanted to tell her about my new approach to getting a job, but before I could she said suddenly, "I think M&M is smoking marijuana." She sounded worried.

I was puzzled. "So what?"

She gave me an incredulous look. "So what? Have you smoked it?"

"Yeah," I said. "You haven't?"

"No!"

"It ain't much. I'd rather have beer any day. I think a lot of these kids just dig it because it's in, it's against the law, and it's supposed to be cool. Me, I think it's O.K., but it sure ain't worth five years in a state prison."

"You won't smoke it any more?" It was a request, not an order, so I answered, "I said I wasn't nuts about it."

Cathy still seemed concerned. "Did you like it? Did it make you want to try stronger stuff?"

"Like acid? Nope, I can't say that it did. But maybe it affects some people like that. At least that's what I read in the magazines."

Cathy sat back with a sigh. "But it's different with you, Bryon. You're smart enough to enjoy yourself without artificial stimulants."

I didn't say anything to this, as I never turn down compliments. She continued, "But M&M, he's so trusting. If he's running around with people who give him grass, he'll take it. If someone handed him LSD and said, 'This is groovy,' he'd say O.K. and take it. I worry because, well, because before M&M always seemed so happy at home; he never seemed to need anything else. But lately he's gotten so much grief for his hair and some of his ideas. I wish Daddy would leave him alone. M&M isn't happy at home now, so he goes other places, I don't know where. I don't even know his friends any more."

"You love him a lot, don't you?" I said, vaguely jealous, feeling a mild form of whatever it was that Mark felt about Cathy.

"Sure, don't you?" Cathy said, amazed at the possibility that someone might not love simple, brilliant, trusting M&M.

"Yeah," I said, because at that moment I loved anything that Cathy loved, because I loved her. I did. I thought it was corny—love is always corny to anyone not experiencing it himself, and even now to me it was corny. But I couldn't help it. I thought about all the times I had said "I love you" to girls I didn't love—to some I didn't even like—and it had been so easy. And now I couldn't even look at her for fear she could tell somehow. It was really weird.

"I think you'd be a good influence on him," Cathy was saying, and I realized I hadn't heard a thing she'd been saying. "I know what," she continued. "Let's pick up him and Mark and go get a Coke over on the Ribbon."

"O.K.," I said. The last thing I wanted just then was to be alone with her; I could easily say something really dumb.

We picked up Mark pretty quick—he was walking home from Terry Jones's house. We had to hunt and hunt for M&M, but we finally found him in the bowling alley.

The Ribbon was a two-mile stretch of hot dog and hamburger stands, drive-ins, and supermarkets over on the West Side, close to where the Socs lived. At night the parking lots were filled with kids sitting on their cars and waving, watching, and yelling at other kids driving by. You could drive up and down the street looking at people, or park your car and look at people. The cops sometimes came along and told everyone to get back into their cars, but the cops were mostly guys who had been patrolling the Ribbon for a long time. The kids had worn them down by being pleasantly smart-aleck and smilingly uncooperative, so unless the kids were openly smoking grass or fighting, the cops were content to sit on the cars with them and yell rude things to chicks driving by.

It was a great place to go to pick up chicks. If you followed a carload of them around for a while, they might pull over and exchange phone numbers with you. Everyone in town went there to see who was going with who and who had what car. If you found someone you wanted to drive around with, you parked your car and left it while you goofed around with maybe a dozen different people in one night. Just the driving up and down was a blast. There had been all kinds of editorials in the paper about it because a lot of pushers took advantage of the filled parking lots, and quite a bit of grass and money exchanged hands there, but mostly it was harmless. Fights down on the Ribbon had really died off in the last year. It had gotten pretty safe, except for drag racing, which caused a wreck or two a week.

"Boy, I hope I see someone I know," Cathy said. "Here I sit, surrounded by beautiful boys."

She gave me a teasing grin. Mark raised his eyebrows. "Well, if you feel that way about it . . ." He put his arm across her shoulders. We were sitting pretty close together because all four of us were in the front seat. Cathy was next to me, Mark on her other side, and M&M was hanging out the window, gravely watching people, waving if he was waved to, yelling back if he was yelled at, always slightly surprised at the crudity of the calls, as if he hadn't heard the same things a hundred thousand times before.

I put one arm across Cathy's shoulders too. She beamed. "It's so nice to feel wanted."

A couple of blondes in an orange Camaro came by on M&M's side of the car and made him an indecent proposition. I thought that kid was going to fall out the window, he was so shocked. The rest of us laughed.

The Ribbon was a two-lane street with an extra lane at the traffic lights for left turns. When we stopped at the light we were in the middle lane, with cars on both sides of us. The blond chicks in the orange Camaro were on our right, and they were still talking to M&M. I didn't catch much of the conversation, but Mark did and he was talking to them too, trying to see around M&M, who took up a lot of the window. On our left was a green outasite Corvette with a couple of guys in it, waiting for a left-turn signal. They looked like real snobs. You can tell just by looking that some guys are snobs. Especially ones with Corvettes. The one on the passenger side glanced over at us and—I still don't understand why—popped off with a really obscene remark. I sat stunned for a minute—the thought of Cathy's hearing such a thing just froze me. Then, so quick I didn't even realize what was happening, Mark reached past M&M, opened the door, pushed M&M out of the way, ran around to my side of the car, and punched the foul-mouthed guy in the nose, literally smashing his nose in. It was their turn to be stunned. Before they could move, Mark was back in the car. He jumped into the back seat and yelled, "Take off!" The light had turned green so I stepped hard on the accelerator. The Corvette was supposed to turn left, and all the cars behind it were honking, so they turned left. I thought maybe they'd come after us —they were older guys, maybe eighteen years old—but they didn't. We drove up and down the Ribbon without seeing them again.

"You're a fast worker," Cathy said. I wondered if she was mad at me because I hadn't been the one to punch that guy. She was my girl friend, I should have done it. I was halfway hacked off at Mark for showing me up.

"Well," Mark said in a mock serious voice, hanging over the front seat, "I get these impulses."

"Impulses to jump out of cars and hit people?" Cathy said dryly, and I realized she didn't think Mark was a hero for what he'd done. As a matter of fact, she didn't think too much of it.

"They hit us first," Mark said, sitting back in the seat. "A hit don't have to be physical. I couldn't hit them the way they hit us without hitting you, too."

I had always known that, in spite of his lousy grades, Mark was every bit as smart as I was. But it was still surprising whenever he proved it to me. Cathy was quiet. Then she turned around and looked at Mark for a long time. "I never know what to make of you, Mark."

"Why make anything of anybody? Why not just take people or leave them?" Mark was in a funny mood. I could tell; I had seen him in that mood before. He was never that way with me, but I'd seen him suddenly turn on people, like a teased lion who's had enough. I remembered the night Charlie was killed—Mark grabbing up the shotgun and firing away. I don't think I could have done that, even if I had known Charlie was dead at the time.

"I don't like being analyzed, baby," Mark said. "So don't."

I couldn't tell him to lay off, because he had a point. Cathy did like to turn everyone inside out and look at him. It didn't bother me, but I could see where it might bug some people.

"I'm sorry," Cathy said, even though she wasn't. I had to say something, so I said, "Let's get a hamburger."

We turned into a big drive-in called Jay's, which was always crowded. It was a set up with a stall for each car and a little deal that had a menu and a button on it. You pushed the button and a voice came out of the deal and said, "Order, please," and you told the speaker what you wanted—in this case it was three hamburgers, one steak sandwich, a cherry-pineapple Seven-up, and three Cokes—and about ten minutes later a chick appeared with the food. It was slightly spooky.

The place was crawling with kids. It was mainly a Soc hangout. There used to be a drive-in over on our side of town where the "hoods" went, but the Dingo was bombed and had burned down so we had started coming over here. Kids were driving through the parking area looking at the kids who were sitting in their cars. It was the same thing that was going on in the street, only on a smaller scale. They had a cop stationed at the drive-in to prevent trouble. He was on a first-name basis with a lot of the kids there; he was a friendly, good-natured cop who didn't mind getting splattered by a water pistol now and then. I didn't much care for him though, due to my feelings about cops in general. I began telling Cathy about the time the cops had beaten me up when I was thirteen.

"You shouldn't have been running around drunk in the middle of the night," she said.

"I never thought of it that way," I said.

"Who would?" came Mark's voice from the back seat. I realized right then that whatever chance Mark and Cathy had ever had of becoming friends was gone. I had already sensed in Cathy the same hostility toward Mark that he had for her. That put me in a really great position.

"Hey, there's Terry Jones. I'm going over to see him," Mark said suddenly. He gave the cop a quick glance—you weren't supposed to get out of your car at the drive-in. They came up with this rule about a year ago because all this switching from car to car was causing fights, and what was worse, cars were left empty in the stalls for hours at a time while the owners were running the Ribbon in someone else's car. This doesn't make money for the drive-ins.

"Mark doesn't like me much, does he?" Cathy said. M&M looked at her, astonished. For the first time I was sick of her honesty.

"You don't like him either," I said.

Not used to having her honesty turned back on her, Cathy was silent for a minute. "I guess we're fighting over you. Isn't that funny?"

"A real riot," I said dryly. I looked across the street, watching some little twelve- and thirteen-year-old teeny-boppers make fools of themselves —smoking, trying to act cool, pushing each other, screaming and swearing so loud I could hear them. I had a sudden recollection of Mark and me at twelve, smoking our heads off, clowning around, hoping someone—usually some little long-haired chick—would notice us and see how cool we were. All of a sudden it seemed like I was a hundred years old, or thirty at least. I wondered if, when I got to be twenty, I would think how stupid I was at sixteen. When I remembered us, it didn't seem possible that we had looked as silly as these teenyboppers, but I guess we had. At least then we weren't worried about looking silly. We were sure of ourselves, so sure we were the coolest things to hit town. Now I wasn't so sure.

That was strange too: in the past I thought in terms of "we," now I was thinking in terms of "me."

"There sure isn't anything to do in this town," Cathy said, breaking in on my thoughts of the good old days.

"We could go to a movie," I said, even though I didn't have the money to go to the movies. Or money to go bowling, or money to go out to dinner, or money to ride go-carts, or to go to the amusement park.

"No, I don't want to go to the movies. There's nothing to do in this town except drive up and down."

"That takes gas," M&M said, "and gas takes money," even though neither Cathy or me had mentioned money.

"Well, let's go drive up and down some more," I said, flipping a switch on the magic dealie that signals a car-hop to appear and pick up our tray.

I was thinking about what Cathy said. There was nothing to do except drive up and down the Ribbon, even though we lived in a fairly large city. It wasn't New York, but for our part of the country it was a good size. All the adults in town screamed about the kids driving up and down, but what did they expect us to do? Sit and twiddle our thumbs like they probably did when they were young? No, thanks.

We drove up and down the Ribbon again—it was getting hard to find a place to turn around. Usually the shopping center at the far end was good for a quick turn-around, but somehow the cops figured out that that was against some law that had been gathering dust for years, so they sat in the shopping-center lots giving out tickets. If a kid got a ticket he immediately went around collecting money from friends and strangers. Usually he got at least a nickle or a dime from each person. I have never known anybody who took advantage of this custom by collecting money when he didn't really have a ticket. This would have been like squealing on someone you saw cheating, or refusing to lend or give or sell your senior theme to some promising junior.

A block beyond the shopping center, under the by-pass, the Ribbon ended as suddenly as it began at a movie theater two miles back. Abrupt and unexplainable. There was another shopping center beyond the bypass but for some reason it was not considered part of the Ribbon, so it wasn't full of cops. We turned around there to head back, which is against the unwritten rules of the Ribbon, but I didn't feel like messing around, sitting in the left-turn lane for half an hour waiting to turn.

"Drive by the hot-dog stand," M&M said, so I pulled in to drive through the parking lot, which was filled with kids sitting on their cars. We got tied up in a long line of cars driving through the hot-dog-stand lot. M&M suddenly got out of the car.

"Where are you going?" Cathy asked.

"I got some friends around here," M&M said. He should have. At least three quarters of the guys out there had hair to their shoulders.

"Well, when can we pick you up?"

"Not ever. I'm not going home," M&M said and walked off toward a group of kids sitting on a station wagon.

There were cars honking behind me so I had to drive on, even though Cathy was yelling, "Stop, we can't just let him walk off like this."

"I'll drive back through," I said, trying to hush her up, because I don't like hysterical chicks. She calmed down right away.

"That little mess. Wait till I get a hold of him."

She didn't though. When we came back through he was gone, and nobody seemed to know where. I parked the car and Cathy and me ran around asking different kids. We drove up and down the Ribbon until one o'clock in the morning looking for him. I found Mark sitting on Terry's car— Terry had gone somewhere with a couple of girls. We picked him up and drove home in silence.

Cathy was crying without making any noise, and, for the first time in my life, I wasn't annoyed with a girl for crying.

Instead, I felt really bad. It was the first time I'd ever felt bad for anyone except Mark.

SEVEN

I went with Cathy to break the news about M&M to her parents and to explain why we were so late. Her father was sitting up waiting for us, and when I saw his face I was glad that I had a real good excuse, even though I was quite a bit bigger than him. Her mother got up and came into the front room in her housecoat. She got real upset when we told her what had happened, but her father said, "He'll be home tomorrow—that kid's been going through this stage for months now."

"It's not just a stage!" Cathy cried. "You can't

say, 'This is just a stage,' when it's important to people what they're feeling. Maybe he will outgrow it someday, but right *now* it's important. If he never comes home it'll be your fault—always picking on him about silly, goofy things like his hair and flunking gym!" She sat down and began to cry again. Her father just looked at her and said, "Honey, I know it's because you're worried that you're talking like this. M&M'll be home tomorrow. He's a sensible kid."

"Then why didn't you ever tell him so?" Cathy sobbed irrationally. "I don't think he's coming home tomorrow. He doesn't do things on the spur of the moment; he thinks things out. He's not going to come home!"

By now two or three younger kids had wandered in, dressed in their underwear or not dressed at all. They got enough out of the conversation to gather that M&M was gone and they began crying too. It was a big mess and I felt really uncomfortable. Mark was waiting out in the car, and, as it was two in morning and I had to go to school in a few hours, I wanted to leave; only I just didn't want to leave Cathy. I wished I could take her home with me. Her father said, "Bryon, thank you for your help. I think you'd better be going home, your mother is probably worried."

I could have told him that Mom never worried about Mark and me—she loved us but let us run our own lives—but I only said, "Yes, sir."

I suddenly noticed that where he wasn't bald his hair was charcoal-colored too and that his eyes, though smaller with age, were the same as Cathy's and M&M's. I wondered if it was strange, seeing your eyes in someone else's face. I was tired and thinking funny.

"Everyone uptight?" asked Mark when I got back into the car.

"Yep," I said. "I don't blame them."

"They don't have nothin' to worry about," Mark said. "Half the kids on the Ribbon are living in someone else's car or house or garage. Shoot, I remember last summer, you and me sometimes didn't come home for weeks—we were bumming around the lake or somebody's house. Remember when Williamson rented that apartment for a couple of months with two other guys? I bet half the kids in town stopped there overnight."

"Yeah, but M&M is just a kid."

"So are we. Nothing bad happens to you when you're a kid. Or haven't you realized that?"

"Youth is free from worry," I said sarcastically. "You've been listenin' to too many adults."

"I don't worry. I'm never scared of nothing, and I never will be," Mark said, "as long as I'm a kid."

"You can get away with anything," I said, because that phrase came through my head whenever I really thought about Mark.

"Yeah, I can." He was quiet. "You used to be able to."

I looked at him, and suddenly it was like seeing someone across a deep pit, someone you couldn't ever reach. It was like the car had widened into the Gulf of Mexico and I was seeing Mark through a telescope.

"What's happening?" I said, half out loud, but Mark was asleep.

M&M didn't come home the next day like his father thought he would. Cathy and I ran up and down the Ribbon every night for a week, but it wasn't fun any more because we were looking out for M&M. We never did find him. We must have stopped sixty million little long-haired kids, thinking they were M&M, but none of them was. I began watching for him everywhere.

I got a job in a supermarket and I did a pretty good job of changing my attitude, outwardly at least. I couldn't help thinking smart-aleck things, but I could help saying them. Sacking groceries wasn't the most fun job in the world, but I was bringing in money. Mark was bringing in money, too, more than he ever had before. I couldn't imagine him stealing all of it, so I figured he must have gone in serious for poker. I never asked him where he got it, and Mom didn't either. Of course, she would never think Mark was getting it dishonestly. Besides, none of us was in any position to turn away extra money.

One night a couple of weeks after M&M disappeared, Mark and me went goofing around by ourselves again. It was almost as if we had never felt a gulf between us, never been separated by something we couldn't see. We drove up and down the Ribbon, trying to pick up chicks and get into drag races, even though our car wasn't all that fast. I was kind of half-hearted about picking up chicks, too, as I was more serious about Cathy than I let on, even to Cathy herself.

"Hey," Mark said suddenly. "Lookit who's over there in the parking lot."

It was Angela and a bunch of other chicks—her type, by the way they dressed and the way they were acting. You can always tell when a girl wants to be picked up.

"Let's pull in," Mark said. He was smiling.

"Sure," I said, feeling, with the old sense of thrill, that something was up, something was going to happen. We pulled into the parking lot, and immediately we were surrounded by girls.

"Outa the way," I said superiorly. "I want to see Angela."

"Bryon!" she yelled, and jumped for me the minute I got out of the car. "Bryon, I'm so glad to see you!"

She was pretty drunk. I let her hug me though, catching Mark's wink. "Where ya been keeping yourself, Angel?" I said. "How's married life?"

She let go with a string of swear words which

told me pretty well what she thought of married life, her in-laws, and her husband.

"I never cared about him anyway. I thought I was having—I mean, I thought I was, but I wasn't— and that's the only reason I married him, the louse." She was half-crying now, between obscenities. "You're the only boy I ever cared about, Bryon."

"Sure," I said. I still hated the sight of her. She was as beautiful as ever, so striking that she could have been a movie star, but I remembered all the trouble she had caused, compared her to Cathy, and hated her. I let her hug me and bawl into my shirt front because Mark was winking at me.

"Angel, let's go for a ride," Mark said. "You and Bryon can talk over old times and maybe I can get some more booze for you."

"Sure," Angela said, always eager for free booze. I couldn't believe she was that glad to see me.

We drove around for a while, Angela telling us all of her problems—her husband didn't have a job, her brothers were both in jail, her old man was drunk all the time, and her father-in-law was always slapping her bottom. I had always taken her family for granted—they weren't so different from most of the families in our neighborhood. But now that I had seen Cathy's home —not rich, not much more than poor, but where everybody cared about each other and tried to act like decent people—the picture Angela was painting was making me sick. I could hardly stand for her to be hanging onto my arm.

At Mark's request I pulled into a parking lot across the street from a liquor store. Mark got out and disappeared. He was looking for somebody to buy the booze. You can't legally buy booze until you're twenty-one in this state, so we always have to get some old guy to buy it for us, usually somebody's big brother. If you can't come up with one of them, there was bound to be some rummy hanging around who was willing to buy it if you gave him a little extra to buy something for himself. I sat in the car and talked to Angela, who had completely given up to tears—it was the first time since I had known her that I had seen her cry. She was a tough little chick. Her eye makeup was running all over my shirt front, but that didn't bother me as much as the way it was running down her face in dark streaks. She almost looked like she was behind bars.

Mark hopped back into the car with some rum, and we got a carton of pop at a one-stop store and took off for the lake. It was too cold to go swimming, but the lake is always a good place to go. There are a mess of them—lakes, that is—around here.

"I get so sick," Angela was saying. "I feel like I can't take it any more, life is so lousy. I'm lousy, everything is lousy. I can't stand it at home. I can't stand it at school, I can't stand it anywhere.

I always thought, hell, I can get what I want. Get what I want and everybody can go to hell. But it doesn't work that way, Bryon. I'm going to hell right along with them. I'm already there."

Tomorrow she would be tough again, hard-as-rock Angela Shepard. Tonight she was tired. And drunk.

She passed out on my shoulder. We were stopped on a little dirt road, one of the millions that run along the lake and through the woods surrounding it. Mark sighed, "I thought she was never gonna shut up. I sure hate to see gutsy chicks break. Destroys my faith in human nature."

"You're never gonna break, huh?"

"Nope," Mark said. He pulled a pair of scissors out of his pocket. "Picked these up at the one-stop." He reached over and began cutting off Angela's beautiful long blue-black hair. Close to her head.

"You ain't gonna cut it all off?" I said, stunned.

"Yeah, I am. Setting up Curtis like she did, gettin' me cracked like that. She coulda had me killed."

"That's right," I said, and suddenly all the hatred I had had for Angela, for her brother Curly, for everything she stood for, came back. I sat and watched Mark cut off all her hair. He tied it all up neatly when he had finished the job. It was a couple of feet long. Even with her hair gone and her makeup streaked all over her face,

Angela was a beauty. She would always be. A lot of good it did her.

We drove home about three that morning. Mark and me finished what was left of the rum. We dumped Angela and her hair in her front yard. She never even woke up. I didn't think she'd remember getting into the car with us, but her girl friends would probably tell her that. She'd know who had cut off her hair.

She wouldn't do anything about it though, because one thing I knew about ol' Angel, she was proud. She'd say she had her hair cut at the beauty shop. She'd say, "I was sick of all that hot mess." She'd never let on.

I started crying on the way home from Angela's and Mark had to drive. Sometimes rum affects me like that.

I was still crying when we got home. We sat on the porch and I cried while Mark patted me on the back and said, "Hey, take it easy, man, everything's going to be all right."

I finally quit and sat sniffing and wiping my eyes on my shirt sleeve. It was a quiet night. "I was thinking . . ."

"Yeah?" Mark said, in the same easy, concerned voice. "What were you thinkin', Bryon?"

"About that kid Mike, the one in the hospital. We talked to him a couple of times, remember?"

"Yeah, I remember. He got beat up tryin' to do a black chick a favor."

"How come things always happen like that?

Seems like you let your defenses down for one second and, man, you get it. Pow! Care about somebody, give a damn for another person, and you get blasted. How come it's like that?"

"You got me, Bryon. I never thought about it. I guess 'cause nothin' bad has ever happened to me."

I looked at him. Nothing bad had ever happened to him? His parents had killed each other in a drunken fight when he was nine years old and he saw it all. He had been arrested for auto theft. He had seen Charlie shot and killed. He had nearly been killed himself by some punk kid he had never seen before.

Nothing bad had ever happened to him? Then I knew what he meant. Those things hadn't left a mark on him, because he was Mark the lion— Mark, different from other people. Beautiful Mark, who didn't give a damn about anyone. Except me.

I suddenly knew why everyone liked Mark, why everyone wanted to be his friend. Who hadn't dreamed of having a pet lion to stand between you and the world? Golden, dangerous Mark.

"You are my best friend, Mark," I said, still a little drunk. "Just like a brother to me."

"I know, buddy," he said, patting me again. "Take it easy; don't start bawling again."

"I sure wish I knew where M&M was," I said, and tears were running down my face again in spite of myself. "I like that dumb little kid. I wish I knew what happened to him."

"He's O.K. Take my word for it."

"You know where he is!" I said. "He's been gone all these weeks and you know where he is!"

"Yeah, I do. If he wanted to come home, he'd come home. Don't worry."

"You gotta take me to where he is, Mark," I said, knowing I sounded like a drunken nitwit—but I couldn't help it, seeing how I was so drunk.

"Sure, Bryon, don't cry. I'll take you there to-morrow. But don't count on him comin' home."

"Cathy is awful worried about him. You know, Mark, I think I'm gonna marry Cathy."

"Come on, man," Mark said, trying to pull me to my feet. "Yeah, marry Cathy and be sure and name all the kids after me. Let's go in the house. Try an' be quiet, O.K.? You don't want the old lady to see you like this. I shoulda known better than to let you drink all that rum."

"Didn't you drink any?"

"Naw, I was drinkin' plain Coke."

"I drank all that rum by myself?" I couldn't believe it. I'm not much of a boozer.

"'Cept for what Angela drank." Mark was helping me up the steps. I was weaving back and forth. If he hadn't been hanging onto me, I would have dropped flat on my face.

"Poor Angel—we shoulda left her alone, Mark. That was a mean thing to do, cut off her hair like that."

"Please, Bryon, for Pete's sake, don't cry any more." He half-dragged me into our room and pushed me onto my bed. I passed out. I could hear Mark moving around the room, feel him taking my shoes off and pulling the blanket up over me, but it was all as if he was real far away, or I was way down inside myself.

"What'd I ever do to deserve you, Mark? Pull a thorn outa your paw?"

"Bryon, buddy, you are as wiped out as I've ever seen you. I think you'd better shut up and go to sleep."

"When did we start runnin' around together, Mark? Remember?"

"We've always been friends. I can't remember when we weren't."

"How come your old man shot your mother? She shot him back, but it was too late because she was dying anyway." I really was drunk, because I had never mentioned that to Mark in all the years I had known him.

"It was me. I was under the porch—I could hear them real plain. And the old man was sayin', 'I don't care, I ain't never seen a kid with eyes that color. Nobody on my side of the family has eyes that color—not on yours either.' And the old lady says, 'That's right. Why should he look like anybody in your family? He ain't yours.' And then they start yelling and I hear this sound like a couple of firecrackers. And I think, well, I can go live with Bryon and his old lady."

"Did you really think that?" I opened my eyes, and the room was turning around slowly. It was making me sick. Something was making me sick.

"Yeah, I did. I didn't like livin' at home; I got sick of them yelling and fighting all the time. I got whipped a lot, too. I remember thinking, This'll save me the trouble of shooting them myself. I don't like anybody hurtin' me."

"I'm glad you came to live with us."

"Me too. Now you really better shut up, man."

"Why you tryin' to shut me up?" I said, making an effort to sit up. It made me even sicker, so I lay back down. "You got a cigarette?"

"Right in the old secret place." Mark pulled back his mattress and got a pack of cigarettes. He always kept an extra pack there. When we were little and didn't want Mom to know we smoked, we kept our cigarettes hidden. It wasn't till much later that we found out she had known about it all along.

I couldn't light my cigarette for some reason. Mark lit it for me and stuck it in my mouth. He sat back on his bed watching me, his elbows on the window sill. I could see the end of his cigarette glowing.

"Charlie, he tried to help somebody out and look what happened to him," I said. This was connected with what he'd said about Mike somehow, but Mark followed my train of thought, just like he always had.

"Charlie wasn't about to let a couple of his

friends get beat up by some hicks. What happened then, well, that was just the way things turn out sometimes."

"Yeah, but listen, Mark, if somebody had said to him, 'Is savin' a couple of dumb kids from gettin' beat up worth your life?' he woulda said, 'Hell, no!' Charlie woulda said that, Mark."

"Sure he woulda said that. But you don't know what's comin'. Nobody does. He sure knew he was taking a chance. Bryon, he musta known those guys had guns. He knew they were rough guys. He took a chance, and he got a rotten break. That's it."

"It doesn't make any sense. Like you gettin' busted with that bottle. A little harder and you woulda been dead."

"But I ain't. This is the way it is, Bryon. Angela Shepard is a tough little chick who set out to get a shy guy who didn't know she was alive, so she sweet-talks some dummy into fighting for her, and I happen to be friends with Curtis, happen to be sittin' on the car with him when the dummy picks the fight with him, and I happen to be a little high. So I step in between Curtis and the punk. Now, if Angela wasn't tough, if she was a nice girl from the West Side—maybe she woulda left well enough alone and given up on Curtis. If Curtis was a playboy like you, he woulda picked her up when she wanted to be picked up. If that kid wasn't so dumb, he would have never taken on Curtis, who is no slouch of a fighter, man, I can tell you. If I had had a date that night, I woulda been somewhere else. But Bryon, that ain't the way things went. You can't walk through your whole life saying 'If.' You can't keep trying to figure out why things happen, man. That's what old people do. That's when you can't get away with things any more. You gotta just take things as they come, and quit trying to reason them out. Bryon, you never used to wonder about things. Man, I been gettin' worried about you. You start wonderin' why, and you get old. Lately, I felt like you were leavin' me, man. You used to have all the answers."

"I can't help it, Mark. I can't help thinking about things. Like Mike and Charlie and M&M and you—it's all mixed up and I can't help it."

"You can help *thinking* about it." He leaned over his bed, reached across the short space that separated us, and yanked my cigarette out of my fingers.

"You're going to go to sleep and burn us alive," he said.

I remember I was going to say, "No I ain't," but I was asleep before I could get the words out.

EIGHT

I was real hung over the next morning. Besides that, I had to get up early and go to work. Mark woke me up. He was a human alarm clock and never needed more than five hours' sleep a night. Me, if I don't get at least nine hours, I feel dead. I felt dead that Saturday morning. I wished I was, anyway, I was feeling so bad that I actually stuck a loaf of bread in a grocery bag and dropped three cans of soup on top of it. Bread always goes on top. In a supermarket this is like the Ten

Commandments all rolled into one. It was a wonder I didn't lose my job that Saturday.

I carried groceries for this one young housewife type, and when I put the bags in her car she handed me her phone number. I was feeling so bad I groaned, "Lady, you gotta be kidding."

Like I said, it was a wonder I didn't lose my job. It was two in the afternoon before the sound of the cash register quit blasting my ears, and it was quitting time before I finally felt I could eat something. This shows you how sick I was.

I had a date with Cathy that night, but she had to work late. I would pick her up at the hospital snack shop at ten. This was fine with me, as I wanted a chance to go look for M&M. Mark knew where he was.

When I got off work, I found Mark sitting in my car.

"I figured you'd want to hunt for M&M," he said. "How's your head?"

"Better. Man, don't ever let me guzzle like that again."

Mark shrugged. "You wanted to. You had to get good and drunk because I was cutting Angela's hair off and you couldn't take it."

I flipped a remark that I had said many times before, but not to him. Even from my side of the car I felt him tighten, getting ready to spring. The gulf was between us again. For some reason, I was hacked off because he didn't need to sleep nine hours, because he wasn't hung over.

"You sound like Cathy," I said.

"Heaven forbid."

"What have you got against her, anyway?"

"What's she got against me?"

"You're a bad influence." I don't know why I said that, because Cathy sure as hell never said anything like it.

Mark was quiet for a minute, then he said something really rotten. I had it coming for what I'd said to him, but he didn't have to drag Cathy into it. I gripped the steering wheel. "You want to get outa this car and have it out?"

"You don't want to swing on me, do you?" It was partly a statement and partly a request. I was quiet.

"I'm sorry," Mark said, and I kept driving. This was as close as we ever came to having a fight.

I followed the directions Mark gave me. We went into this old part of town which used to be a really classy place maybe thirty or forty years ago, with these huge old houses that were probably a big deal when they were built. They just looked gloomy now; most of them were divided into flats.

On Mark's say-so I pulled into a driveway in front of one of them. There was a sign hanging from the porch ceiling that said "Love" in red-and-green letters.

"He's here?" I asked, because I wasn't sure what was going on.

"Last time I was here he was." Mark got out of the car. You can tell when somebody is familiar with a place. Mark had been here many times before. "Come on."

I got out of the car, wondering what in the world Mark could have been doing here. Mark didn't knock, he just opened the front door and walked in. I followed him. The whole inside of the house was freaked out with posters. A girl with long, streaked, blond hair, wearing blue jeans and a paint-splattered shirt, was lying on a beat-up couch. She had the deadest, most colorless face I had ever seen.

"Hello, Cat," she said to Mark. She knew him; she didn't call everybody "Cat."

"Peace, baby," Mark said. I tried not to laugh. I dig hippies O.K.—I mean, they've got some great ideas, but sometimes it was funny.

"Freaked out?" Mark said politely, as if he were saying "How are you these days?"

"'Way out, man." She was staring at the ceiling so intently that I glanced up there, just to make sure the answer to the universe wasn't written across it. If it was, I couldn't see it. Maybe she could.

Mark stepped over a stringless guitar and went upstairs. I stumbled after him, looking around. Somebody was in the kitchen singing. Each of the steps was painted a different color. It was a good effect, but they were awful dirty.

Mark stepped into a bedroom. There were

about six or seven kids in it. One kid was lying on a bed watching his fingernails. The others were sitting cross-legged in a circle, talking about some book. I hadn't read it so I didn't get the conversation, but these kids were not dumb. They were all in blue jeans and old shirts and fringed vests. A couple of them were smoking grass.

"Hi, Cat," a guy with a beard and a flowered shirt said.

"I'm looking for M&M," Mark said. "You seen him?"

"Baby Freak? He ain't been around today. The kid's flying, man. He's going to crash."

"You didn't let him take anything, did you?" I said. This may have been against house rules, as nobody had said anything to me yet, but this place was getting on my nerves.

"There isn't any 'letting' here," this fat chick says. "We're free."

I looked her over with the practiced eye of a playboy and popped off with something really good. Then I raised two fingers and said "Peace." This seemed to earn their forgiveness, because they all went back to their literary discussion.

Now the kid on the bed was painting his fingernails with green water-color.

On the way out we passed the blond chick. She was reading a book and smoking grass.

"You seen Baby Freak?" Mark asked.

She shook her head. "Sorry. See you around, Cat." Even sitting up she looked dead.

When we got back into the car I said, "You dating her?"

"Sometimes. Like the lady said, they're free."

I thought about that a long time. I am the first to admit I've got hang ups. I don't think I'd ever consider myself really free.

But I'm not sure I'd consider them free, either.

"Just because it ain't your bag, don't knock it," Mark said, after we had driven in silence for a while."

"I didn't say anything."

"Grass, rum, both are a high."

"Yeah, well, listen, man, rum's going to maybe get me a weekend in the drunk tank. Grass could get me five years in the pen."

"That law ain't necessarily right."

"It's the way things are." I was puzzled. I had never known Mark to smoke pot. I wondered why he was defending it.

"I don't smoke it, so quit worrying," Mark said, reading my mind as usual. "I just don't like to see you judging people."

"What the hell is bugging you? I didn't say anything."

Mark was quiet. Then he said, "You remember when the Socs used to come through here looking for somebody to beat up?"

"Yeah."

"You remember when me and you beat up that hippie kid in the park?"

"Yeah," I said.

"I'm a tough punk, Bryon, but I ain't dumb."

We drove the rest of the way home in silence.

I picked Cathy up at the hospital. I didn't tell her about going to the hippie house to look for M&M. I didn't see any sense in getting her all upset. After all, I hadn't found him.

We drove up and down the Ribbon, then stopped by the park on the way home. This was becoming standard procedure. I was getting more and more serious about Cathy, and this was really strange for me. I had always had a love-'em-and-leave-'em attitude. Even with Angela, I guess it was more a pride thing than a love thing. I still hadn't told Cathy I loved her though. It was like my never thanking Charlie for letting me use his car. It was something I just couldn't do when it meant anything.

"Hey, Cathy," I said, while we were on the way home. "If I got a ring, would you wear it?"

"Yeah," she said. That's how we started going steady.

After I dropped Cathy off at her house, I headed for Terry Jones's place. I was supposed to pick up Mark there, but when I got to the house, nobody was home. Terry's parents were out of town for the weekend, which normally ~t it was party-and-poker time at the Jones-~gured everybody had gone out scouting for booze and broads, so I sat down on the front steps to wait.

It was a cool night, but not too cool. It was getting to be spring. It had been a real weird winter. Last fall Mark and me had thought just alike, as one person; now we couldn't even talk. Charlie had been alive and griping about our Coke bill. I had been a hustler, both with pool and chicks. M&M had been reading *Newsweek* and getting his kicks baby-sitting. Now everything was different.

While I was sitting there, smoking and thinking, a car pulled up. I thought it was some guys coming to party and so forth, so I didn't pay any attention. The four guys were standing right in front of me before I came to and realized that two of them were Tim and Curly Shepard.

"I thought you guys were in the cooler," I said pleasantly, just like I didn't know they were here for the sole purpose of stomping out my guts.

"We're out now," Tim said. He scared me. He was what I would call a rough guy. Curly was mostly mouth, but Tim backed up anything he said. He really was a hood. I know most people call any kid from over here on the East Side a hood, but Tim really was.

"I guess so," I said, still smoking, not blowing my cool. If I kept them talking long enough, maybe Mark and Terry and God knows who else would show up.

"Seen Angela lately?" Tim said. Curly was

keeping his mouth shut—even he was awed by his big brother. There was something about Tim Shepard—his scarred face, his fighter's slouch, the flickering of his black eyes—that really let you know he meant business.

"Yeah, as a matter of fact, I saw her over on the Ribbon last night, and she went for a drive with me." I decided I didn't need to drag Mark into this—it was plain they weren't worried about him.

"No kidding? Did you know Angel got her hair cut this morning? At least that's what people say. She told me something different."

I was sweating. I could feel it running down my back and wetting my palms, and my cigarette was shaking, so I ground it out on the porch. But I sounded calm as I said, "What's she telling you?"

"She says you got her drunk and cut her hair off. That the truth?"

"Yeah, that's the truth, and I'm sorry it happened." I decided to tell it straight for once, without all this hedging and playing the game. "It was a rotten thing to do and I'm sorry."

"You ain't half as sorry as you're going to be," Tim said, and the two guys I didn't know rushed me, pinned my arms, and held me while Tim and Curly took turns punching me.

I passed out finally, but not as soon as I had hoped I would.

When I came to, Mark was wiping my face off with a wet rag.

"Bryon, you O.K.? Don't move, man."

I bit back a groan because I could tell there were other guys in the room. Normally I wouldn't have to knock myself out playing the tough guy for just Mark, but I did have a rep to keep.

"What happened? Who did this to you?"

"Shepards," I said finally, but it hurt to draw the breath to say it. Something was stabbing me in the sides. My whole face was throbbing and I couldn't open my eyes. They were swollen shut. There was a funny taste in my mouth—I guessed it was blood.

"You want to go to the hospital?" Mark asked. He sounded so worried that I felt sorry for him.

"No," I said. I didn't want to go anywhere. I felt that if I moved I'd fall apart. "Can I stay here?" I figured I was in Terry's house somewhere. I could tell I was lying on a bed.

"Sure, man, you stay here." I recognized Terry's voice. "Brother, you look like you been through a meat grinder."

"That's what it feels like too," I said, even though this witticism cost me more stabbing pains in my sides. A reputation is one hell of a thing to have; you got to kill yourself to keep it.

"I'll call the old lady," Mark said. "Then we'll go look up the Shepards."

"Mark!" I said. "I want to talk to you, personal-like."

"Sure, buddy. Clear out, you guys." And because he was Mark, they obeyed him.

"Listen, it hurts like hell to talk, so I'm only goin' to say it once, an' I don't want to argue."

"Sure." Mark's voice sounded puzzled. I wished I could see him; I knew he wasn't going to dig what I had to say. I could tell he was sitting on the edge of the bed, and I reached for where his hand should have been and caught it. "I don't want anybody to fight the Shepards."

"What?"

"I don't want to keep this up, this getting-even jazz. It's stupid and I'm sick of it and it keeps going in circles. I have had it—so if you're planning any get-even mugging, forget it." I was trying to keep my voice from trembling with pain, but not only did talking hurt my sides, it was killing my face.

"I got you, Bryon," Mark said after a silence. "You just take it easy." He left to call Mom, and I heard him yelling at the rest of the guys to keep the record player down. He stayed all night on the other side of the bed, guarding me.

think about was Mike's getting beat up for driving a black girl home. I kept remembering him saying he didn't hate the guys who did it. Well, I didn't hate the Shepards either. I tried to explain this to Mark as we drove home. I was so wrapped up in what I was trying to get across to him that I was startled when Mark suddenly burst out, "Whatdaya tryin' to do to me, Bryon?"

"What?" I said, confused. Mark had turned white and his voice was shaking as if he was about to cry. I couldn't believe that; I had never seen Mark cry except from physical pain.

"How do you think I feel, man? You won't let me get the Shepards for you, and here you go givin' me this song and dance about how you don't feel bad about gettin' beat up. You think I don't know they beat you up for something I did? And here you are, practically sayin' you had it comin', when it was me who cut Angela's hair, it was me who planned it, and me who did it— and it's you who gets beat up for it. Like that damn fool, Mike, he feels like he had it coming, feels guilty for something somebody else did. Man, that is sick! How do you think I felt, finding you lying there in the yard? I knew it was the Shepards. If they had killed you it woulda been my fault. That is eating me up, Bryon, and you won't even let me get even for you."

He was crying. I just went sick inside. "Mark, it ain't your fault. It's just that I'm sick of fighting. I'm sick of this circle of beating up people and getting beat up. It's stupid." I reached over and gave him an easy punch on the shoulder. "I ain't dead, man; there's nothing to worry about."

Mark took a deep breath, and, even though his voice was normal, he was gripping the steering wheel so hard that his knuckles were white. "I don't know what's the matter with me. I never worry about 'what if?' I never did until me and Terry came home and found you lyin' there smashed up. Then I think, 'what if?' and look what happens to me." He shrugged. "You don't want to get even with the Shepards, that's your business."

We just couldn't get through to each other. He didn't understand why I didn't dig fights any more; I didn't understand how he could accept everything that came along without question, without wanting to change it.

Mom nearly had a fit when she saw me. She was well by then, back at her job. I almost gave her a relapse. I had never been so messed up. A black eye she could take, stitches in my lip she could take, smashed ribs she could take, but not all at the same time. I was feeling so lousy that I didn't mind her fussing at me. I pretended that it was her who made me go to bed, but I was glad to be there.

"You want me to call Cathy?" Mark asked after I had been put to bed.

"Yeah—you mind?" He could get to a pay phone and I couldn't.

"Sure, I mind. Beating up the Shepards would be easier. But for you, buddy, I'll do it." He gave me his famous Mark grin. "I know she'll be glad to hear from me."

I tried to grin back at him, but it was difficult. It's pretty lousy to have the two people you care about most hate each other.

I must have dozed off when Mark left. I felt pretty bad—the painkiller shots had worn off and I was running a fever. I don't know how long I was asleep, but when I came to, Cathy was sitting next to the bed.

"Hi, Bryon," she said, and her voice and her face were so serious that for a dazed second I couldn't figure out if it was Cathy or M&M. I really felt dizzy and drunk and confused.

"How do you feel?" she asked, when I couldn't say anything; I just lay there and looked at her stupid-like.

"Oh, all right," I said, which made a lot of sense. "I'm glad you're here."

"Are you?" she said, and she was crying. There, I had both her and Mark crying within twenty-four hours. I must be really something.

"Cathy, I am really glad you are here," I said. "I love you."

"O.K.," she sobbed. "O.K." Then she reached over and held my hand. I took a quivering breath and looked at the ceiling. That hadn't been so hard after all. If I could do that, maybe there were a few other things I could take care of.

"Well," Cathy said finally, gulping back her tears, "your mother says you'll be all right in a couple of days." She sort of half-laughed. "You just look so awful, Bryon."

"You look great," I said. She didn't really, I guess, because you never do see a girl who looks good while she's crying except in the movies, but to me she looked good.

"I'll be fine in a day or two; then we can go find M&M. I got a lead on him," I said. My mind was clearing up.

"Really?" Like I hoped, this took her mind off me for a little while, and like I hoped, not much.

"Yeah. Mark says he's seen him at this hippie commune-house."

Cathy looked shocked. "One of those free-love places?"

"I don't think that's the right word for it." I couldn't help grinning. "Anyway, he's been staying there. I went over to look for him yesterday, I think"—I was still a little confused as to what day it was, or what time. "He wasn't there then, but maybe we can find him. Don't worry, the place wasn't that bad. He could have been in worse places."

"All right." She smiled at me like I knew everything on earth, like whatever I said went, and it really made me feel good. "We'll go look for him when you get better."

She reached over and gave me a quick, light

kiss. Because of the stitches in my lip, this hurt.
But not much.

I took a couple of days' sick leave from work—
I didn't want to go to work looking like some
prize fighter. But as soon as I was able I took
the car and went for a drive by myself. I had
been thinking about a lot of things. Cathy, Mark,
M&M, and Charlie. I drove around for two hours
before I finally made up my mind.

I drove out to the cemetery, the cheap cemetery where people who don't have money get
buried. I hadn't gone to Charlie's funeral, but I
knew where he was buried.

I finally found his grave. This was not easy
since there wasn't much of a marker. There
weren't any big headstones in the whole place.
I went and stood in front of his barren grave.
No flowers, no nothing. Just the place where what
was left of Charlie lay. I said out loud, "Thanks for
letting me use your car, Charlie. Thanks for saving
my life."

This wasn't hard to do. I wished I'd done it
when he could have heard me. I don't know, maybe
it was a dumb thing to do, but I sure felt better.

I picked up Cathy two nights later and we
went looking for M&M. Mark had gone out somewhere; he was spending more and more time
away from home. Mom was worried about him,
I could tell. By now she was also bugged about
where he was getting the money he kept bring-

ing home. I still figured he was doing some serious poker playing, but I didn't want to tell Mom that, as she didn't have too high an opinion of poker, or gambling in general. Me getting mixed up on that pool-hustling business hadn't done much to glorify gambling, either.

"I just love your mother," Cathy said as we left the house. She and Mom were getting along pretty good. This was fine with me, as I dug her parents O.K., too. Right now Cathy was hacked off at her old man; she blamed him for M&M's running away. But I liked the guy.

"Most people do," I said. "She knows everybody within twenty miles of here. The mailman brings her all the stray kittens he finds, and the neighborhood grocer gives her free cat food."

We were feeling real good driving to the hippie house. We laughed and kidded and horsed around all the way. I figured we had a pretty good chance of coming home with M&M this time.

There were two Volkswagen buses parked in the driveway of the old house; I knew they belonged to the hippies because of the flowers and slogans painted on them. One read "War Is Unhealthy for Children and Other Living Things." Really bright.

"This is where he is?" Cathy sighed. "I still can hardly believe that baby is living in a place like this."

I guess big sisters always think of little brothers as babies, no matter how old they are. "Maybe it was good for him," I said. "Maybe being on his own made him grow up a little." I only half-believed this; I had always had a good opinion of M&M's mind, but being smart ain't being mature, as I have often proved. "Anyway, we can't be sure he even wants to come home with us."

"If he doesn't, Daddy is going to call the cops and have them bring him home. He doesn't want to, but he keeps saying M&M has had his fling, and it's time he came home. This is my only chance to get him home without dragging the police into it."

"I didn't know that. Well, let's hope he comes with us. Maybe I could slug him and carry him home."

Cathy laughed. "No, let the cops do it if it comes to that. I'd rather have him hate the police than you."

We walked up to the house. There were kids on the porch, just watching the street. I stopped to talk with a Biblical-looking guy.

"I'm lookin' for Baby Freak. He around?"

"Yeah, he is." The guy was staring directly into my eyes. He had friendly, trusting eyes. "Are you a friend of his?"

"Yeah, a good friend. This is his sister."

Cathy gave him the big smile she won me with. The guy smiled back.

"He's upstairs, I think." Suddenly the guy looked worried. "He's been floating for a couple of days now."

"Oh, no kiddin'," I said, keeping my cool, and Cathy followed my example.

"Talk to his travel agent," the hippie said. "He's the cat with the red hair, inside."

"Travel agent? What's that?" Cathy whispered as we went in. I didn't want to tell her, didn't want her to feel the sudden cold waves of fear that I was feeling, so I said, "I don't know."

We found who we were looking for—a big, heavy guy with fire-colored hair, beard, and mustache.

"We're looking for Baby Freak," I said. I was beginning to see why M&M had acquired this other nickname: most of the kids there were at least seventeen or eighteen, with a lot of college-age kids. It was a real crowded place, but now I can't remember what everyone was doing. At least some of the kids were smoking grass; you could tell that by the smell. I was hoping the place didn't get raided while we were there. You can get busted just for being at a place where people are smoking pot.

"Yeah?" Red said. "Man, that kid is on a bad trip."

Cathy made a funny, yelping little sound.

"Some of these freaks have been dropping acid. Baby wanted to try it, so I sat with him. Bad trip, man, really bad. He's calmed down a little now, but all day today me and some of these other cats been holding him, keeping him from jumping out the window."

I felt like I was going to throw up. Cathy was as white as a sheet. "Can we see him?" she said, in a tiny, expressionless voice.

"Sure."

We followed him up the stairs. He led us to the same room Mark and I had gone to the last time we were there. This time no one was there except the blond chick, who was curled up on the bed asleep, and someone huddled in the corner. To my surprise, Red walked over to the huddle. "Hey, man, there's people here to see you," he said softly.

"Are they spiders?" The person didn't raise his head, but the voice was M&M's.

"No, man." Red laughed gently. "They're squares."

M&M looked up, and I hardly recognized him. His hair was to his shoulders, he was a lot thinner, he was dirty, and the expression on his face was one I had never seen on him before—suspicion.

"M&M, baby, it's me—Cathy." Cathy kneeled down in front of him. He was staring at her, not seeing her.

"Square spiders?" he said, and his face was contorted in fear. "I don't want to see any spiders."

"It's me, Cathy," she said again. "Your sister. Don't you want to go home?"

"I went to my stomach," M&M said in a high, unnatural voice. He was talking too fast. "I went down into my stomach and all these spiders came out. I never knew there were spiders in my stomach. I was there ten years, and all that time these spiders kept chewing on me. They were big spiders."

Cathy choked back a sob. "Baby, what have you done to yourself?" she said in a whisper.

He seemed to see her. "Cathy? I screamed and screamed and screamed, but nobody came to help me." He was shaking. He didn't look right. He looked sick. "I kept trying to get back, but the spiders held me down. Held me down and chewed on me and the colors went in and out. I listened to the colors and they were screaming too. Red and yellow screamed loudest. The spiders were eating them too."

"He kept trying to jump out the window," Red said. "All day. We took turns holding him down."

What did the guy want, a medal? He had given him the stuff in the first place.

"Cathy," I said. "We ought to take him to the hospital."

She looked at me quickly. "Hospital?" Then she nodded. "Let me call Daddy first." She looked at Red. "Do you have a phone I can use?" She followed him out of the room.

"There was this other color," M&M said to me seriously but half-afraid, as if he thought I'd turn into a spider any minute. "I don't know its name; it told me but I forgot. It said I was being paid back for all the carrots I ate. I didn't know—I thought—I didn't know about the carrots before. I don't think it was my fault." He was crying, tears were pouring down his face, but he hadn't changed his expression. He looked so thin and scared, not a bit like the M&M I knew. "Do you think I should be paid back for something I didn't know about?"

"No," I said, clearing my throat. "I don't think it was your fault." I put my arm around him and held him. He was shaking real bad.

Cathy came back. "Daddy's going to meet us at the hospital. Can you carry him?"

"Yeah," I said. I picked him up easily; he couldn't have weighed more than ninety pounds.

"I'm so tired," M&M said. "I was gone so long, and I didn't have any sleep." I carried him down the stairs and out of that house. Nobody made any move to stop me. Nobody seemed to care.

Cathy drove us to the hospital. Halfway there M&M started suddenly and screamed, "Where am I?"

"It's O.K., kid, you're going to be O.K."

"Where am I?" he was screaming in terror. "Why don't I know where I am?"

I was just sick. I didn't know how Cathy was managing to drive the car. I never felt so bad before. I just held onto M&M. There wasn't any sense in trying to talk to him. I felt then that he was as much my little brother as Cathy's. That's how bad I felt.

Mr. Carlson was waiting for us at the hospital.

We drove right up to the emergency entrance, and there he was. I got out and picked M&M up again, but I didn't have him for long. Mr. Carlson took him and carried him into the hospital, holding him very close, very tight.

M&M was telling him about the spiders.

TEN

We stayed there at the hospital until the doctor could talk to us. He couldn't tell us much—physically M&M would recover, but mentally . . .

"Will he always be like he is now?" Cathy said. She had really been brave—no crying, no hysterics. Only by the tense, tight way she was ripping the hem out of her shirt was she showing how bad she was shook.

The doctor replied, "I have no way of knowing. He might get better, or he may have lost his mind forever. Either way, I don't believe he'll ever be completely the same. LSD is a powerful drug, people react to it differently. If these kids would only . . ."

I tuned him out. I won't listen to sermons. Besides, I was hacked off at that doctor. He shouldn't be saying things like that. He should be saying that M&M would be fine, that tomorrow morning he would be the same again. Couldn't he see how what he was saying was tearing Mr. Carlson to pieces? Couldn't he see what it was doing to Cathy? What kind of a doctor was he, anyway?

"I want to drive you home," I said to Cathy.

She shook her head. "I don't want to go home. I want to stay here."

"Cathy, I want you to go home," Mr. Carlson said. "You can't do anything here and I want you to be with your mother when she hears about this. M&M will be asleep for a few hours. I'm going home in an hour or so. Wait until I get there before you tell your mother." His voice broke. "What are we going to tell her?"

"Come on," I said, putting my arm around Cathy, guiding her to the car.

"Wait a minute," Mr. Carlson said. "Bryon, I want to tell you how much I appreciate all you've done. I'm really proud of you, son."

That was the first time any man had ever called me "son" without making me mad. I didn't know what to say, so I just nodded to him and gave Cathy a squeeze.

In the car Cathy broke down and cried. I drove to the park and stopped. I held her while she cried. She was almost hysterical. I was crying too. I couldn't stand seeing her hurt like that. I just couldn't stand it. "Don't cry like this, baby," I said. My voice was shaking. "Cathy, don't. It won't do any good."

"Oh, my God," she sobbed. "What if he's lost his mind forever? He was such a sweet kid, the sweetest damn kid in the whole world."

This was the first time I had ever heard her swear. I tried to think about this fact, to focus on something like that before I lost control and became hysterical too. "He's going to be all right," I said. "He'll be just like before."

"No he won't." Cathy was trying to stop crying now. "He won't ever be the same." This set her off crying again. My shirt front was soaked clear through. She just hung onto me and cried while I patted her head. Finally she sat up. "I love you so much, Bryon," she said. "I don't know what I'd have done without you."

"I love you, too, baby," I said. This was getting easier to say. "And don't worry about what the doctor said. He's one of those hippie-haters. M&M will be O.K., I know it."

"I'd better go home now," Cathy said. "I have to be there when Mamma hears. Oh, this is just going to kill her."

I let her out at her house, but I didn't go in.

I figured this was a family matter, and I wasn't a member of the family yet.

I was surprised to see how late it was when I got home. Mom was asleep. I went into my room and lay down without bothering to turn off the light. Mark wasn't home yet. I was tired. I felt empty and drained. Nothing can wear you out like caring about people. I was tired, yet I knew I wouldn't be able to sleep. I closed my eyes, but I kept seeing pictures: all these people were spinning around in my head—Mark and Charlie and Mike and Angela, Cathy and M&M and Mr. Carlson, and Tim and Curly Shepard. Life had seemed so simple once, now it suddenly seemed so complicated. I could remember a time when my only worry had been paying Charlie the three bucks I owed him. Things used to be simple and now they weren't. I wanted a cigarette bad. I half-heartedly searched my pockets, but I knew I didn't have any. Then I remembered Mark's spare carton and rolled off the bed and reached under his mattress. I felt something strange and pulled it out. It was a long cylinder-like thing. I unscrewed one end and all these pills came rolling out.

I am not dumb by any means. I have never used drugs except for a couple of tries with grass, but I knew what they looked like. I looked at this bunch of pills—there were hundreds of them, and it was like a machine in my head went *click*,

click, click. And it came up with an answer I didn't want.

Mark was selling this stuff. This was 'way too many pills for anybody to have if he was just taking them himself, and besides, I would have noticed something different about Mark if he had been taking them. You can't use drugs and not show it—I knew too many kids who were users not to know that. Mark was selling. Mark was a pusher. That was where he was getting his money. That was why he had known about the hippie house; that was why they had known him; that was why he had known where to look for M&M.

M&M. Cathy.

M&M was in the hospital, and maybe he was messed up for life—and Mark was selling the stuff that made him that way. Maybe this wasn't LSD, but it was a step in that direction, and God only knows what all Mark had been selling. I thought about that blond, deadlooking chick and about M&M screaming about spiders and about Cathy half-hysterical with grief. I thought about Mr. Carlson and the bitter doctor, and the whole mess was swirling around in my head, and it felt like it would burst wide open.

When I thought about the cause of all this misery, I became very cool. I very calmly called the cops. M&M had lost his mind and Cathy was hurting, and I did something about it. Then I sat down on a chair in the front room and waited. It seemed only a minute later when Mark came in.

"Hey, still up?" he said. Then he stopped. "What's the matter—Bryon, you look awful! What is it?"

I held out the cylinder.

"Oh," Mark said, after a pause. "You found them, huh? Well, don't worry, buddy, I don't take them. I have a good enough time like I am."

"Just how are you, anyway?" I said.

"What?" Mark said, confused.

"M&M is in the hospital—acid trip. They think he may have lost his mind."

"Man, that is awful. That poor kid." Then he looked at me. "Bryon, don't look like that. I said I don't take them. Don't you believe me?"

"I believe you," I said dully.

"We needed the money, you know. I tried getting a job, but with my police record nobody'd hire me. Then I met this guy on the Ribbon—he set me up. I figure I don't have to take it to sell it, so what's the worry?"

"M&M—" I began, but I was too tired, too numb to talk.

"Is that what's buggin' you? Listen, I didn't sell M&M anything. He got it from somebody else. Lookit, Bryon, they're going to get it from somebody if they want it, so why can't I make some money? I never forced it on anybody. I never tried to talk somebody into using drugs so I could make a buck."

He could have talked all night and I wouldn't

have changed my mind. This was wrong. For the first time in years I thought about the golden-eyed cowboy who had been Mark's father. Was Mark a throwback? To what? I wondered tiredly why I had never seen it before: Mark had absolutely no concept of what was right and what was wrong; he didn't obey any laws, because he couldn't see that there were any. Laws, right and wrong, they didn't matter to Mark, because they were just words.

"Bryon, what is it?" Mark cried suddenly. "Listen, if it bugs you that much I'll quit. I'll stop selling if you don't like it. Shoot, I never thought it would bother you. I sort of thought you knew about it."

Don't drag me into this, I thought. Don't try to make me out to be blind, just because you are. Aloud I said, "I called the cops," and I felt as if I was talking in my sleep. Mark went white.

"What?" he said softly disbelievingly. "What did you say?" We could already hear the siren. "Bryon, you know what something like this would do to me with my record. Bryon, tell me you're lyin'." Mark was pleading desperately.

I thought maybe he would run for it, but he didn't. He just sat down in a chair opposite me. He was white and his eyes were black with a rim of gold around them. He looked the way he had when he had been clobbered with that bottle. "Bryon," he said quietly, like he was trying hard to understand, like he was totally confused, like he thought maybe I would answer in a foreign language, "why are you doing this to me, buddy? Bryon, just tell me."

I couldn't tell him. I didn't know.

The police arrived, and of course Mom woke up. She didn't know what was going on. She could only stand helpless in the kitchen doorway while the police questioned me, rounded up the drugs, and slapped handcuffs on Mark. They advised Mark of his right to remain silent, and he did. He just stood there, quivering, watching me while I told the cops the things that would put him behind bars for years.

Then a cop said, "Let's go, kid," and it seemed to dawn on Mark what was happening. He looked quickly from the cops to me and cried, "My God, Bryon, you're not gonna let them take me to jail?"

Didn't he know I had just put him there? The cop jerked Mark around and shoved him out the door. Suddenly it was deadly quiet—just the distant siren and Mom's quiet sobbing.

I went into the bathroom and threw up. I was sick.

ELEVEN

The next morning I really thought that I had dreamed the whole thing. I thought I had had a nightmare, one I only vaguely remembered. It seemed a long time before it finally got through to me what had happened. Then I was tired and sick, and I wondered why people didn't die from being so mixed up.

Why had I turned on Mark? What had I done to him? I tried to remember how shook I had been about Cathy and M&M, tried to justify what I had done. But I didn't know now. If I had asked Mark to quit selling pills, he would have. I didn't have to do what I did. Last night it had seemed the only right thing to do. Now Mark was in jail. It would kill him. It would kill him.

It would kill him.

"Bryon, are you going to work?" It was Mom. I was sitting on the edge of the bed, holding my head in my hands. It felt like it was going to burst wide open.

"Mom," I said wearily, "what have I done? You don't hate me, do you?"

She came in and sat down on Mark's bed. "Bryon, you are my only child and my son and I couldn't hate you. I love you."

"You loved Mark, too," I said, only beginning to realize how this mess was going to affect her. Mark, her stray lion, behind bars.

"Yes, I loved Mark and I still do. But you are my son and you come first. What Mark was doing was wrong. Maybe the juvenile authorities can help him."

"You know they can't." I was too worn out to play games—let's pretend everything will turn out all right, let's pretend it's all for the better.

"We'll just have to make him understand it was wrong and that what you did was for his own good."

I took a good long look at her. She was my mother and I loved her, but there wasn't any sense in carrying on the conversation. She was

tired and hurting, too, but she had hope and I
didn't and we couldn't talk.

"I gotta get ready to go to work," I said.

"Bryon, don't hate yourself," Mom said, but
that was easier said than done.

I went through the day mechanically, numb,
and hardly knowing what I was doing. I had a
rep as a wisecracker and a clown, so this got me
a lot of ribbing, but I hardly heard it. I was glad
to get home and lie on my bed, smoking one cigarette after another, not thinking—scared to think.

I heard someone at the door, but since Mom
answered, I didn't pay any attention.

"Bryon, you have company," Mom finally
called.

It was Cathy. It occurred to me with a shock
that I hadn't thought about her all day long.

"Bryon, your mother told me what happened.
I'm so sorry." She looked tired and nervous but
I couldn't work up any sympathy for her.

"Are you?" I said "Why?"

"Bryon!" she said, tears jumping to her eyes.
"You know I know how you feel!"

"Oh," I said. "No, I hadn't realized that."

She was quiet, bewildered. I knew I was hurting her, but I couldn't seem to stop myself. It
was as if I was outside myself, watching while
someone named Bryon Douglas hurt his girl
friend. I couldn't stop him, and I wasn't much
interested in the first place.

"How's your brother?" I said. Suddenly it was

just some brother of hers in the hospital, not M&M, not my friend, not somebody I too cared about.

"He seems better—but I don't know, he's still mixed up."

That makes two of us, I thought sarcastically.

"I thought"—she swallowed, she was a proud person and it was hard for her to be humble—"I thought maybe you'd come up to the hospital today or call me or something. Then your mother told me what happened."

"Aren't you glad?" I said. "You never liked Mark—you thought he was beautiful, but you didn't like him. Aren't you glad he's out of the way?"

"Bryon, why are you doing this to me?" she said, and suddenly I could hear Mark, as plain as day, saying, *"Why are you doing this to me, buddy?"*

"I'm sorry," I said. "I can't talk today, Cathy. I'll call you tomorrow."

"O.K.," she said, still puzzled and hurt but no longer humble. "Call me tomorrow."

I wasn't going to call her tomorrow and she knew it.

I wondered impersonally why I didn't love her any more. But it didn't seem to matter.

Mark had a hearing, or a trial, or whatever—I never paid any attention to the formalities. I had to testify. I did. I hadn't seen Mark since they had come to get him. He looked relaxed and amused, tipping back in his chair, glancing over everyone in the courtroom with an easy, almost friendly expression. When I was questioned about my relationship with Mark and answered, "We were like brothers," Mark laughed out loud. When he was questioned, he admitted selling drugs and shrugged. I think it was his attitude that made the judge go hard on him, even though by then judges were beginning to crack down on pushers. Mark was only sixteen; he had always been able to talk his way out of anything. But this time he didn't try. When the judge sentenced him to five years in the state reformatory, he didn't even change expression. I felt like someone had knocked the breath out of me, and I heard Mom's little cry of protest, but Mark got to his feet and casually strolled out with the officers. He hadn't looked at me once.

The next months were a blur—I went to school and went to work and went home and studied. I ended up with straight A's that semester, something that surprised me more than anyone, because I couldn't remember a thing I had studied. I didn't date. Once, at the drugstore, I ran into M&M.

His hair was much shorter than it had been in years, and he was still thin.

"I haven't see you around in a while," he said.

"Yeah, I been busy. How ya been?"

"O.K.," he said, but he looked half-scared, and

his old expression of complete trust and intent interest was gone entirely. He looked like a little kid—I had forgotten he was just a little kid. "But, I don't know—It can come back, they told me. I could have a flashback, it could come back. And if I ever have any kids—something about chromosomes—they could be messed up. I don't think I'll ever have any." He was quiet for a minute. "I don't remember things too good any more; all my grades are shot."

I couldn't help feeling sorry for him. He had been such a bright, sweet kid. I remembered the time—it seemed years ago—when Mark and I had teased him about wanting a large family. Well, that was taken care of.

"You used to go with Cathy, didn't you?" he said. The poor kid, he was really confused. He was reading a monster comic.

"Yeah, for a while."

"She liked you better than anybody," he said.

"I know it. She's dating some guy named Ponyboy Curtis now. She likes him O.K. too."

I couldn't feel any anger, any jealousy, any anything except a halfhearted hope that they would hit it off together. Any grudge I had ever held against Curtis was gone, so was any feeling I had ever had for Cathy. It seemed impossible that I could once feel so emotional about someone, and then suddenly feel nothing.

"I'll see you around," I said. But I hoped I

wouldn't. M&M made me sad, and I hadn't felt anything for so long—it was slightly scary.

I spent that summer working full time and trying to get to see Mark at the reformatory. But every time I went they told me that Mark was causing trouble at the reformatory so he couldn't have visitors. I got promoted from sack boy to clerk. I didn't come to work hung over and I didn't give the manager any lip. I seemed to have become a mixture of things I had picked up from Charlie, Mark, Cathy, M&M, Mom, and even obscure people like Mike and the blond hippie-chick and the Shepards. I had learned something from everyone, and I didn't seem to be the same person I had been last year. But like a mixture, I was mixed up.

Angela came into the store once wearing short shorts and a tight blouse. It was funny, but she looked even better with short hair. I guess I'll never see a girl as good-looking as she is. She came through my counter, staring at me coolly, daring me to say something. Poor little chick. I didn't hate her any more than I loved Cathy. I felt sorry for her.

"How've you been, Angel?" I said, but not smart-like. I really wanted to know.

"Well enough. I hear you dumped little what's-her-name on Curtis. Well, they deserve each other."

I just shrugged and rang up her stuff. She was

going to be bitter all her life, and all that beauty was wasted.

"You know, I'd thought for a long time you were really low, Bryon," she was saying, "but what you did to Mark really proved it."

"Angel, you look really good with short hair," I said, and I don't know whether or not it scared her, but she shut up.

One night when I was lying on the floor reading a book, Mom came in and sat down. "Bryon, you got even with Mark for Cathy, then you got even with Cathy for Mark. When are you going to stop getting even with yourself?"

I rolled over and got up and went for a drive. I couldn't talk to Mom, especially when she was telling the truth.

Finally, at the end of August, I got to see Mark. He couldn't leave the reformatory, so I had to go in. He had been in so much trouble that the authorities considered my visit a last-ditch effort to straighten him out. If it didn't work, they were going to send him to the state prison. They told me they hoped I could influence him.

They didn't say how.

I thought we'd have to talk through a wire dealie, like you see in prison movies, but instead we were left alone in a room which I remember as strangely empty.

"Hi ya, buddy," Mark greeted me. "Slumming?"

I couldn't speak. I had a real bad pain in my

throat. Mark had changed. He had lost a lot of weight, but somehow it had stretched his skin over his bones and slanted his eyes. He hadn't lost his looks, but exchanged them. He looked dirty somehow, and hard, things I had never seen in him before. His strangely sinister innocence was gone, and in its place was a more sinister knowledge. He seemed to be pacing, like an impatient, dangerous, caged lion.

"How goes it?" I managed finally. "What's the action like in here?"

"If I told you how it was in here," he said, "You'd be sick." There was a silence. Then he continued, "I didn't have to see you. I wanted to, though. I had to make sure."

"Make sure of what?"

"Make sure I hated you."

I suddenly remembered that time, so long ago, when Cathy had looked at Mark and for a moment I had hated him. I wondered what it felt like to experience that feeling all your life—to hate the person you loved best.

"Mark . . ." I began miserably. "Mark, I didn't know what I was doing . . ."

"Can it, buddy." He glanced around. "Groovy place, ain't it? Seems like home now."

"I hear you've been causing trouble."

"Yeah. I don't seem to be able to get away with things any more."

I thought I would break down and cry then, but I didn't. "Listen," I said, "you straighten up and they'll let you out early on probation or parole or whatever it is, and you can come home. I'll get you a job at the store—"

"Like hell you will," Mark said, in the same, easy, pleasant voice he had used all along. "I ain't never goin' back there again. When I get outa here, you ain't never going to see me again."

"We were like brothers," I said, desperate. "You were my best friend—"

He laughed then, and his eyes were the golden, hard, flat eyes of a jungle animal. "Like a friend once said to me, 'That was then, and this is now.'"

I broke out in a sweat and was suddenly glad of the walls and the guards and the bars. I think if he could have, Mark would have killed me.

I haven't tried to see Mark since then. I heard in a roundabout way that he was sent to the state prison. I've just been sort of waiting around for school to start, not much caring whether it does or not. I don't seem to care about anything any more. It's like I am worn out with caring about people. I don't even care about Mark. The guy who was my best friend doesn't exist any longer, and I don't want to think about the person who has taken his place. I go over everything that happened last year, trying to figure out what I could have done different, what I would do different if I had the chance, but I don't know. Mostly I wonder "what if?" What if I had found out about Mark some other time, when I wasn't half out of my mind with worry about Cathy?

What if I hadn't met her in the first place, would I still have grown away from Mark? What if M&M had had a good trip instead of a bad one? What if someone else had turned Mark in—would there still be hope for him?

I am too mixed up to really care. And to think, I used to be sure of things. Me, once I had all the answers. I wish I was a kid again, when I had all the answers.